THE CUNNING DEGREE

Pretty Qi

Copyright © 2022 Pretty Qi

All right reserved. No part of this publication may be reproduced distributed, or transmitted in any form or by means, including photocopying, recording, or other electronic or mechanical methods, without the prior written permission of the publisher, except in the case of brief quotations embodied in critical reviews and certain other noncommercial uses permitted by copyright law. For permission requests, write to the author, addressed "Attention: Permissions Coordinator" at madamqi@sina.com

ISBN: 978-1-957144-10-8 (Paperback)
ISBN: 978-1-957144-11-5 (EPUB)

Library of Congress Control Number: 2022902598

Any references to historical events, real people, or real places are used fictitiously, Names, characters, and places are products of the author's imagination.

First paperback edition February 2022
Printed in the United States of America

Edited by Pretty Qi
Typesetting services by Asian Culture Press

Asian Culture Press
444 Alaska Avenue,
Suite #AZF046,
Torrance, CA 90503
United States

Dedication

With this book, I would like to illuminate some secrets in the world, stand up for justice.

Preface

The author is about 50 years old, currently living in a country, and has been working for more than twenty years. In these long years, she has encountered many hypocritical issues in life.

Although the book is written in a memoir-style and is positioned as a work of fiction, many stories described in this book reflect real-life events.

This book is different from conventional novels. There are fewer character dialogues, as the author created the book to mirror reality, so the dialogues in the book should also reflect real-life events.

The writing and publication of this book have exposed some shady events. This may cause displeasure for some administration departments as they might want to maintain their positions. Here, the author would like to express her sincere goodwill. She hopes that this book will act as a reminder to the administration departments of all countries worldwide. The people should not be bullied even though they do not have any governing power, as fairness and justice in society should not be repressed.

The author also hopes that the country will become more civilized and just.

This book has been written and shaped to a large extent by the information exchange in this technological era. The author is deeply convinced that it is a blessing to live in an age where technology has developed, and each of us is no longer blinded by information barriers, thanks to collective efforts in technology by mankind.

The author has a lot of fans and admirers in the United States, and the messages they sent to her made her feel warm and supportive. The author also hopes that no matter where you are, you will be able to feel the spirit and warmth of fairness and justice.

Author

Table of Contents

The National College Entrance Examination (NCEE)

This is a country located beside the Pacific Ocean. The United Nations has classified it as a developing country based on its economic and scientific advancements.

Most territories of this country are in the temperate zone, so it is neither too hot nor too cold. The temperature is moderate, and the four seasons are distinct. There are many rivers and lakes. The coastal area is vast and rich in resources, giving rise to many thriving cities.

Modern technological advancement gave rise to many bustling and charming cities. There are high-end office buildings in the towering central business districts, shopping malls, and commercial streets with colorful advertisements, intoxicating people in the beauty of material things. The temptation of food is irresistible in the supermarkets with a dazzling array of food. The transportation is well planned, and the subway runs every few minutes in more than a dozen lines, providing transport to ordinary office workers. Overhead roads also travel without traffic lights or speed restrictions, providing convenience to the middle class. There are also large and busy international airports with daily flights and frequent inflow and outflow of passengers. Aircraft from all over the world, such as Boeing and Airbus, fly across the Pacific from here.

Modern cities continued to attract people with their charm. The population in large cities increased and grew denser, often reaching 10 million or even 20 million people. Larger cities have more than 10 million people, while metropolitan cities have more than 20 million. Resources and spaces are limited to survive in such a city. Everyone knew the basis of survival they needed to enjoy a high quality of life here.

Many countries have a relatively long history, and the same is true for this country.

Having a long history means that tradition is ingrained in society, and the mainstream cultures have influenced people's thoughts, guided their behavior, and created social norms. This society values learning and believes that those who excel in learning would make a good official or leader.

This belief originates from the imperial test system thousands of years ago, where scholars participate in the national imperial tests from small counties to large provinces. In each test, outstanding students will be selected to take the final test in the capital city. Sometimes, they would even participate in the imperial test in the palace, an opportunity to showcase their talent in front of the emperor. If they are ranked among the top in the test, they would have a chance to be appointed to the cabinet. It would be a noble opportunity and a meteoric rise to fame. Who wouldn't envy that?

Times have changed, and civilization has progressed. The imperial system has long been abolished in the present era. The country is now a republic, where every citizen is equal before the law and people are free. What standards can be used to determine if a person is excellent or mediocre? Higher education. University education is used to evaluate if someone is good or average.

In this country, going to university and receiving a full-time education is no longer simply about getting a decent job after graduation. In a society bounded by traditions and societal norms, going to a university and having a good degree is not only a proof basis to get job and make a living; it is also a symbol of one's identity and social status in society. It would be even better if the university they attended were the first-class universities among the country.

Therefore, attending university and obtaining a degree in full-time higher education is seen as an important event that everyone and their family eagerly anticipates.

There are more than 2,000 universities in this country. Every year, the number of students who graduate from high school and want to enter the universities would reach hundreds of thousands or even millions of people. Hence, the education department organized the NCEE, "the National College Entrance Examination". It is large-scale unified and comprehensive examination involving the high school students in the country, only be established once a year. Students must take 6-7 subjects and go through a series of difficult and complex subject examinations. The NCEE is highly influential examination held across the country at the same time and is revered by the public. It is an important examination in life and is often regarded as "the examination that determines the fate."

The NCEE is a competitive examination with universality and fairness, it is designed to select the outstanding and comprehensive students according to their ranking. The ranking is based on total score of the examination accumulated from 6-7 subjects. After the scores came out, the students were ranked based on their total scores. Later, according to the ranking, the admission score lines at all levels were announced, then, the students filled out their intentions which universities they wanted to attend, they would be admitted into universities with different levels of excellence for full-time higher education.

There are different levels of fame and reputation between various colleges and universities. Just like in the United States, Harvard, Massachusetts Institute of Technology, Stanford, Yale, Princeton, and other well-known universities are different from the rest. To achieve the goal of creating world-class universities, the education department focuses on developing 39 first-class excellent universities. The 39 universities are the best among the other universities and became the ideals and goals of the students who took the NCEE.

The status of the NCEE stood like a myth in the hearts of the public. Every student will need to take 6-7 subjects in the NCEE. The NCEE is like a filter, screening thousands of students who studied hard for more than a decade with its difficult and complex questions. To this day, almost everyone who took the NCEE knew its prestige.

The NCEE is a competition for every student, where they compete each other, and weaker students will be eliminated from the competition.

The number of students being admitted to universities had nothing to do with the direct scores. The admission is based on the student's final ranking, the ranking among hundreds of thousands or even more than one million students in a state or province. A student must obtain a high rank to qualify for university. In other words, if you are the examination candidate, you will need to compete with hundreds of thousands of people during the NCEE to gain admission to university. Could you have enough confidence to take the ranking?

The NCEE is a battlefield. There are often hundreds of thousands of candidates in a certain region such as a state or a province. The admission rate for the 39 excellent universities in this region is often less than 20%, usually only around 10%+. Using the ratio of 20%, only 2 out of 10 students will be admitted into excellent universities. It is useless no matter how hard other students' study. For most students, it is necessary to study hard to improve their final ranking to be admitted into university. Many students put up slogans before the examination, such as "As long as you don't die when you study, you shall study till death," "NCEE, we challenge!" etc. Nevertheless, the competition in the NCEE is fierce, and many students fail to enter excellent universities. The NCEE is a turning point in life; every student's ranking in the list is as if the future status in society.

Everyone wants to have a degree that could provide nice impression to society, so they can get good job and income, also get to the good social class. Since the NCEE is challenging and competition is fierce, some families choose to avoid the fierce competition and not participate in the NCEE. They choose to study abroad and become international students, even if the fees are exorbitant. (The school fees for an undergraduate degree abroad can cost about 200,000 – 300,000 US dollars). This is also the reason why more and more students decided to study abroad for an undergraduate degree because the NCEE is difficult, and it is even more challenging to enter a prestigious university.

In the present era, the situation has somewhat eased due to the expansion of the admission quota in universities. The problem was even worse in the 80s and the 90s. In the 90s, the university admission quota had yet to expand. The university's admission rate was low, the examination questions were complex, and the number of students who passed the examination was minuscule. The country valued university students very much and would arrange proper jobs for them. For instance, the government would provide job once the students graduated from universities. Hence, the competition for the NCEE was fierce, and hundreds of thousands of students competed at the same time. They were ranked by the total scores of 7 subjects and competed for university admissions. The competition reached a cut-throat level where each point of the score could eliminate dozens of students. If the student was careless and falls behind by a few points of the score, the student would drop behind hundreds of students in the ranking position. They would be eliminated and might not have the opportunity to go to university. Many students studied hard for years. But due to their carelessness in examination, they were regrettably eliminated from the brutal competition. Meanwhile, those who managed to enter elite universities were praised by society and crowned with the reputation of "Heaven's Favor."

CHAPTER TWO

The Best Degree

Qiqi is the main character of this book. Qiqi obtained her degree in the 90s, and it was very prized in that era. It was a small achievement that Qiqi had gone through the grueling NCEE and got her current job.

Even though she didn't get it from a prestigious university, Qiqi was proud of her degree.

She was born in a large city in the central region, the city was built near water. There is a large river flowing in the middle of the city, and the city flourishes.

Competition exists when there are many people. Qiqi could recall that she studied in an outstanding high school. Back then, the common norm in society was to enter an outstanding high school in order to pass the NCEE. Hence, the competition began during high school.

Qiqi resided in the capital city of a province, and it was an important economic and cultural center in the central region of the country. Although it was not as prosperous as the other first-tier cities along the coast, its quality of education was excellent among the country.

Besides having several universities, the city also has an excellent high school that is ranked first in the country. The students in the school are not only exceptional in the NCEE, but they are also elites in every aspect.

For instance, the winner student of two gold medals with perfect score in the International Mathematics Olympiad came from this school.

Also, during the height of the pandemic, students could only study at home. Still, the top scholar for the NCEE came from this school. The student had obtained an excellent grade for language (including the essay, only 4 points were deducted from full marks). It was amazing as it was an unprecedented record, and no one had ever scored such excellent result.

The vice-premier of the State Council had personally visited the school and praised the school's quality education.

What was the extent of the excellence of the students in this school? Passersby would often show admiration and sometimes even fear whenever students walked out of this school with the school emblem. They would often whisper among themselves, "Look, it's a student from that school! Look at the emblem! These are people who will be great in the future." Qiqi (a student from that school) would smile whenever this happened. She knew that she was excellent. She used to rank first in class in language and won awards in essay competitions, which was why she was able to enter the excellent school and enjoyed the prestige. Nevertheless, being a girl, she wasn't very fit and had health problems, which had affected her studies later.

With a righteous, bright, and independent character, Qiqi became a person who would uphold her integrity and never follow the crowd.

Qiqi's health issues became more and more apparent since her sophomore year in high school. Recurring pain due to inflammation in her body worsened, and the doctors told her that it couldn't be cured as it could only be alleviated with medication.

The preparation of 7 subjects simultaneously, highly intensive studies day and night took a toll on Qiqi's health. The amount of schoolwork had affected her physical health. She had no choice but only to review the important subjects. She persevered and had no complaints even though she had foreseen that she wouldn't be able to do well in the examination. She knew that she had a good foundation, so she used it to take the examination, hoping that she wouldn't fall behind the ranks. Life is hard, and she could only face the hardships head-on.

She finally passed the admission line and received a university admission notice. It wasn't a prestigious university, Qiqi was once the most outstanding student and was ranked first in language during school, due to her health condition, she only managed to obtain a degree from a regular university. It was a pity! But Qiqi felt lucky as the NCEE was harsh.

Nevertheless, Qiqi is a talented person. Even though having a degree is important, what is more, important to Qiqi is to accumulate knowledge and skills over the years. People spend years at work, and they must work for decades. They won't be able to persevere in life if they don't have real talent.

Qiqi knew the importance of having a degree as it represented the benefits and interests one could obtain in real life. The government had previously issued wage-level guidance. Different levels of education would correspond to different amounts of basic salary. For instance, the amount of basic salary would increase as the level of education increased, e.g., associate degree, undergraduate, master's, and Ph.D.

Qiqi understood the importance of income and benefits in life. However, she felt that society placed too much importance on it. Qiqi couldn't accept the idea of obtaining a degree for the sake of personal interests. She grew up in an elite and cultured family and was brought up with good values and traditions. To Qiqi, it is more important to maintain an upright character in life.

Qiqi's uncle is an elite and an expert who had received an allowance from the State Council. Previously, he was given the opportunity to meet the Vice Premier face to face. Her cousin brother is a news reporter and is now residing in Toronto, Canada, enjoying a good life.

Her father was a director at the senior management level of a large state-owned enterprise. Her mother was a senior lecturer at a polytechnic college. She is a well-educated and respected intellectual.

Her parents graduated from full-time universities in the early days. During that time, the standard foreign language used in this country wasn't English, it was Russian. (Note: The official language in the country is a language with stroke order. English and Russian are considered foreign languages in this country.)

Even now, her parents often speak Russian to each other in their free time, igniting Qiqi's curiosity. Not to be left out, Qiqi often read out aloud in English. The atmosphere was interesting because of the common presence of English and Russian. Qiqi knew that she was brought up in a good family and was confident about her family background as she had more insight than an average person.

Qiqi had a little secret that she would never tell anyone, and she even calmly believed that it was unnecessary to talk about it as it might destroy other people's self-esteem and self-confidence if she did. Qiqi had a copy of a degree from the country's most enviable and outstanding university. It is a science degree from Jinghua University. In this country, the status of Jinghua University is unshakable and revered by everyone. It is the best university in the country.

The copy of the degree is a testament to Qiqi's excellent talent. The original degree belonged to a male classmate who was Qiqi's admirer in high school. He is exceptional in mathematics, physics, and chemistry. He often represented the school and participated in various mathematics and science competitions. When the mathematics teacher encountered complex and challenging problems, he wasn't ashamed to discuss them with the male classmate to solve the questions.

They got along well with each other as classmates in school. The male student knew that Qiqi was an upright person and talented in language. He kept his feelings hidden until the examination ended and after graduating from high school. Only then did he confess his love for her. Qiqi didn't accept his love as she thought it wasn't appropriate since he was younger than her. Plus, she had just graduated from high school, and she didn't want to enter a relationship at that time. She rejected him as she thought they were both too young to enter a relationship.

Later, the male classmate graduated with a master's and Ph.D. degree. When he finished his studies and came back to meet Qiqi, Qiqi already had a boyfriend. The male classmate was disappointed and had nothing to give Qiqi, so he made a copy of his degree from Jinghua University and gave it to Qiqi as a keepsake, hoping that it would accompany her. Qiqi cherished the degree very much. She stored it carefully as she knew that it was the fruit of hard work and years of study.

Qiqi had never told anyone about this, and neither her father nor mother knew about it. The copy of the most remarkable degree accompanied Qiqi quietly as the years went by.

CHAPTER THREE

The Foreign Language School

Qiqi studied commodity management at university. After graduation, the government assigned her to work in the Commodity Management Bureau, which is a national agency.

Before her official day at work, Qiqi's mother had a heart-to-heart talk with her. She spoke affectionately, "From now on, you'll start work officially. You'll need to work hard and be dedicated to your job." Qiqi nodded, and her mother continued, "Don't overwork yourself. Remember to take a break from time to time." Qiqi smiled. "Okay, Mommy."

After a moment of pause, her mother pondered and shifted her eyes away. A moment later, she turned and glanced at Qiqi's smooth and youthful face. Qiqi's face was full of radiance and hope. Her mother said softly, "Getting along with the people in the unit is not as easy as it seems. Working in a unit is different from being at home. You'll need to be careful." Qiqi wondered and tilted her head quizzically. She couldn't understand what it meant, so she asked, "Mummy, what do you mean?" Qiqi's mother sighed and slowly muttered something Qiqi could never forget in her lifetime. It is as if it was a warning. "There are all kinds of people out there with different diathesis and characters. Remember, you shouldn't be too trusting. You need to have a clear judgment." Qiqi widened her eyes in shock, only to return to normal after a long time.

Qiqi worked at the headquarters in the city. She was assigned to one of the business segments. The department head took Qiqi on an office tour and assigned a position for her. Then he introduced her to other colleagues, and all of them applauded to welcome her to work. Qiqi looked around, and the office was relatively spacious. There were more than ten colleagues, and all of them were sitting in their cubicles. Qiqi nodded politely and waved to greet them. After introducing herself, she went back to her seat.

Her colleagues stared at her quietly. Some of them were delighted. A moment later, a bespectacled man came over and greeted her. "Hello, which university are you from?" Qiqi told him her university and major, which the colleague then nodded in approval. "Good!"

When she was about to leave work, a middle-aged woman came over and asked her with concern, "Do you have a boyfriend? Do you want me to introduce you to someone?" Qiqi was flustered by the question and was caught off guard. "Oh, I don't have one. No, sorry, I have a boyfriend. Thank you for your concern."

Her parents laughed when she told them about it. In fact, Qiqi had no definite suitor at that time. She just thought that she was there to work, and it wasn't good to mix personal matters with work. She had no interest in love. All she had in her mind was to work wholeheartedly.

Qiqi's job gave her a lot of exposure to different categories of commodities. She needed to review and check the commodity classification information submitted by each sub-department. She would check if there were any errors with the information submitted and whether it was categorized accurately into the corresponding category. For example, should air conditioners used in cars fall under the category for air conditioners or minor parts for cars? That is something that requires expertise.

Although Qiqi is good at language, she chose to take science subjects during high school and even after she entered university. During her high school years, her language teacher made it a point to talk to her when the students were separated into Science and Arts streams. His surname was Xu. He wore thick glasses and was very old. From the opposite side, one could see the transparent rings on each glasses sheet. Qiqi knew that the thick glasses Mr. Xu wore indicated his long years of experience in teaching. He was a responsible teacher. At the same time, he had a very loving heart and was loved by students.

At that time, when Qiqi went to the teacher's office, Mr. Xu got up tremblingly to greet her. He then gestured for Qiqi to sit opposite him. He raised his arms to adjust the position of his glasses. Then, he looked at Qiqi with affectionate eyes and slowly said, "Qiqi, since you're good in language, you shouldn't choose science stream. You should choose the arts stream; it would be more beneficial to you in the future."

Qiqi froze as soon as she heard Mr. Xu. What he said was true, and language is a subject that Qiqi could master and use freely. However, to Qiqi, science is natural science. The reason why the country is lagging in the development in recent times is mainly due to the weak foundation in natural science. Qiqi is not a person who learns only for her personal benefit. This was even though she knew that she had to take the NCEE and obtain a high score in total. In the NCEE, natural science subjects such as chemistry and physics account for many marks in science stream subjects. If she chose to study science, she would lose her advantage in the score.

Qiqi understood Mr. Xu's good intentions, so she contemplated briefly before she replied with certainty, "I think everyone should learn about science. That's the foundation of the country." Mr. Xu sighed. "When you start working in the future, the unit will care if you have gotten your degree from a famous university. No one will care if it's a science or arts degree."

Qiqi is passionate about science. To Qiqi, science is as mythical as the stories in books. Science theories such as the photoelectric effect and electronic escape, nuclear fusion in the sun, crystallized chunks of carbon indicating that planets are diamonds fascinated Qiqi. Also, she learned that the Earth is a lucky planet because it isn't too near or too far from the sun. There is a moderate amount of light from the sun, enabling the creation of life on Earth. Knowledge and theories in natural science are a myth for Qiqi. It is inspiring and deepened her love for knowledge. The process and purpose of learning is to obtain actual scientific knowledge, and the end goal of education shouldn't simply be to obtain a degree. Qiqi believes that everyone who genuinely loves science would have the same opinion.

For that reason, Qiqi often went to the bookstore on her rest days to read and buy books, hoping to improve her knowledge and insight in greater depth. Qiqi thought that reference materials at work and course knowledge obtained at university weren't sufficient as time changed and new commodities were appeared. As a professional manager, she should keep up with trends and familiarize herself with different commodities.

There was a distance from where Qiqi lived to the bookstore. On the way to the bookstore, she would pass by a relatively secluded road. She looked out from the bus window; the whole road looked secluded as it was lined with rows of tall and huge French Sycamore trees. The buildings next to the road were blocked by the trees and branches, making it impossible to see. However, it didn't seem like residential buildings for civilian use; it looked like unit office buildings. Qiqi thought to herself, "What kind of building is this? Who would build something in such a secluded area in the city?" As she was deep in her thoughts, a closed iron gate and the sign on a stone pillar caught her eye – 'Foreign Language School.' "Oh, it's a school." Qiqi thought. She then recalled that the outstanding high school she had attended was situated in a prominent location on the main street. Parents and students could see it immediately.

Qiqi pondered. "Foreign Language School?" She recalled scenes where she spoke foreign languages with her parents at home. All students must learn a foreign language no matter what major they take in university. Her parents studied at the university much earlier than her. They studied Russian at that time, but the government later changed the policy, and university students were made to study English. This meant that every university graduate could speak some English. This is because English has become an important language to communicate internationally and is used universally. Hence, the government would need to follow the trend as well.

What is the purpose of a foreign language school? Why did the administration department set up independent foreign language school under the condition of every graduate would learn a foreign language? Moreover, even if people fail to enter university, foreign language is an important subject in secondary school. It is a compulsory subject for the NCEE. In other words, everyone who had attended middle school would need to learn a foreign language. The law in the country stipulates that everyone should attend junior middle school. It meant most of the adults on the street had at least some foreign language knowledge.

The existence of foreign language school she had just seen was a little strange, "Why does that school exist?" The question had been hanging in her mind.

In the times of the last century, smartphones weren't available, and computers weren't used widely. Qiqi wouldn't be able to find information from the Internet.

When she went home to visit her parents on the weekend, Qiqi told them about her journey to the bookstore. Then, she asked her parents, "I saw a school. The name of the school is Foreign Language

School. Why is there a separate school for foreign languages only? Don't all of us learn a foreign language in school?"

Her parents looked at each other confusedly and shook their heads. Her dad contemplated briefly and replied, "I've never heard of any foreign language school that is independent of other schools. Everyone studied in a regular school and took the NCEE to enter universities. The university students from all over the country also took the NCEE to enter the university." "Yeah, your father is right. He used to be the class monitor at that time." Her mother added.

"Well, let's put the school aside." Qiqi stopped.

Qiqi stopped thinking about it and continued her life calmly. She worked on weekdays and bought groceries on weekends. Sometimes, she would go to the bookstore, and sometimes, she went to visit parents.

After working for several years, the colleagues in her unit grew more and more concerned about her private life. Seeing that Qiqi always came and left work alone, an enthusiastic colleague tried to set her up with marriageable men. Qiqi was embarrassed and couldn't bear to reject her anymore, so she agreed to meet up with the man that her colleague had introduced.

CHAPTER FOUR

The Bookstore

The first meeting between marriageable men and women is called a "blind date" in this country. Qiqi was going on a blind date. She was nervous as she had never been on blind dates and was a little restless on the afternoon before the meeting.

The appointment was set after work on a Friday, and Qiqi wore beautiful clothes to show her respect for her colleague and the man she was going to meet.

After work, they went to a restaurant together with the colleague as the middleman.

The man wasn't tall and was relatively thin. His overall mannerism was rather average.

Qiqi's colleague introduced them to each other, "This is Liu, my neighbor." Then she introduced Qiqi to Liu. "This is Qiqi, a colleague in my unit." They nodded toward each other awkwardly.

When they were seated for dinner, the colleague was ecstatic, as if she was the one attending the blind date. During the meal, she kept praising both. First, she praised how polite and gentle the man was. He had no bad habits such as smoking or drinking, and he was a fine man. Then, she went on to compliment Qiqi for her dedication at work. She vouched for their characters as she knew both well.

The awkward meeting clouded Qiqi's mind, and she felt unease. She didn't know how to express herself in that awkward situation. It felt like she was forced to participate in the blind date. She was uncomfortable as the interaction was only one-sided. She only listened to her colleague and couldn't express herself.

After dinner, Qiqi's colleague suggested that the two of them go for a walk outside alone. Qiqi had never taken a walk with a stranger before. She used to go for walks with her parents by the river. She could recall blue petunias blooming beautifully by the river.

They strolled, and the man wanted to find something to talk about, but he couldn't think of anything to say as the colleague had blabbered everything during the dinner. They walked in silence for about half an hour. Qiqi was tired and felt that it was pointless to continue. So, she stopped walking and thanked the man. After all, he paid for dinner. The man replied politely. As it was getting late, Qiqi said, "That's it for today. I'll leave now." The man quickly replied, "Let me send you home." Qiqi thought that too much time would be wasted to go back and forth, so she declined and thanked him again.

She laid in her bachelor pad during the weekend, deep in thought.

She was already 25 years old. Although she was comfortable being single, it seemed to go against social norms. It was frustrating having to participate in countless blind dates.

She had to solve the problem at hand.

So, Qiqi went to the gift store, bought two gifts, and had the merchant wrap them up delicately.

She went to work as usual on Monday. On Tuesday, when it was almost time to leave work, Qiqi brought the gifts and went to meet the colleague who had set her up on the blind date. She expressed her gratitude and complimented the man. Then, she explained that they seemed incompatible with each other. She thanked her colleague for setting her up on the blind date. Qiqi's colleague was embarrassed when she saw the gifts and heard Qiqi's explanation. She was stunned for a moment. Then, she said, "Let me know if you want me to set you up with someone again." Hurriedly, Qiqi nodded.

Everything was calm for now.

She carried on her life, working and resting as usual. However, a thought popped up in her mind. "Should I start dating?"

On her rest day, she continued to go to the bookstore. There weren't many people in the bookstore. Except for the audiovisual section that was usually lively and packed with people, there weren't many people in the books section.

Qiqi bent down and picked some books. Most of the books she picked were science books. She looked at the synopsis and the contents. Then, she checked if there were illustrations, preferably colored, so it was more intuitive. Time passed quickly. The knowledge in the books gave Qiqi a deeper understanding of the world and life. She felt more confident; it was probably the power of knowledge.

One day, when Qiqi was reading, she suddenly felt as if someone was walking toward her. That person stopped just as he was getting closer to her. Qiqi thought he was an acquaintance, although it shouldn't be her colleagues since she had never met them in the bookstore before. The activities she usually heard her colleagues talk about on their rest days were grocery shopping, entertainment activities, and gatherings.

Qiqi raised her head, quietly sensing for a while before turning toward that person. It turned out to be a young man, seemingly of a similar age to herself. He looked kind and well- mannered. Cautious and polite, he asked, "Excuse me, do you work for the Commodity Management Bureau?"

In normal situations such as on the streets or in a noisy shopping mall, Qiqi wouldn't have paid much attention to him. At most, she would nod and leave without many words. But since she was in the bookstore and everyone was here to read, she dropped her guard, nodded, and looked at him.

The man was delighted. "Oh, then I remembered it correctly."

"Huh?" Qiqi didn't understand what he meant. The man proceeded to introduce himself, "I'm Jack Chen. I'm working in a foreign company. I saw you when I accompanied my colleague to the Commodity Management Bureau to submit an order." "Oh." Qiqi tried to recall, but she couldn't remember if she had met him before. Qiqi's department is responsible for reviewing the commodity categories. If there's an issue with the categorization, the company would be asked to submit further information. Her other colleagues would have dealt with him.

Both Qiqi and the man seemed more relaxed. Qiqi placed the book back on the table and walked out slowly after looking at the time. The man followed suit and continued to chat excitedly, "I graduated from university and majored in engineering. I visit the bookstore often to read about engineering to keep up with times." Qiqi smiled and thought that he was a chatterbox. But she was surprised to know that he graduated from the same university as herself. But they didn't know each other as he was more senior than her.

They chatted as they walked. Qiqi thought it was a coincidence that he was her college senior. It was a pleasant chat.

After that, Qiqi would often meet him when she went to the bookstore. He would come over and chat with Qiqi enthusiastically. Gradually, Qiqi grew feelings for Jack.

One day, when she was working in the unit, someone came to submit the documents. Her colleague dealt with them. Suddenly, she heard a familiar voice. When she turned to look, she realized that it was the man that she had encountered in the bookstore. He was with his colleagues. Stunned, Qiqi was a little surprised when she saw him.

He nodded to Qiqi from a distance and didn't come over to talk to her.

Later, when they met at the bookstore, Qiqi asked him, "Why did you come to the bureau that day?"

He replied thoughtfully, "I'm afraid that you wouldn't believe me, so I accompanied my colleagues to your unit to verify my identity."

Qiqi smiled and opened her heart to him. She seemed to take a liking to Jack.

They slowly grew closer. Jack was delighted when he knew that Qiqi was his junior in university. Qiqi also let down her guard and called him "Alumnus Chen."

From that day onwards, they made frequent trips to the bookstore and went for meals in the fast-food restaurant beside the bookstore, as if they were friends.

Moments like this lasted for more than a year. Qiqi thought that having someone around to talk to was better than reading alone. Perhaps, this was the feeling of companionship.

One day, after the trip to the bookstore and a meal, Mr. Chen suggested they go for a walk by the river. Qiqi agreed.

The weather was comfortable and pleasant. The river was wide, and the air was fresh. A cool breeze blew across, and Qiqi couldn't help but stretch out her arms to embrace the fresh air.

Full of energy, Alumnus Chen said, "Watch me."

He loosened his jacket and took a big step forward on an open space. Then he stood upright firmly and placed both of his arms above his head. After that, he did a somersault and flipped in the air before landing on the ground steadily, just like the gymnastic performance on TV. Everyone near them cast admiring glances, and Qiqi couldn't help but clap.

After that, Qiqi quickly stepped forward to support him and asked with concern, "Are you okay? Are you hurt?" Mr. Chen looked at Qiqi intently. Then he grabbed her arm and asked formally, "Can you be my girlfriend? I'm almost thirty now." Qiqi blushed. She pondered and nodded since she was reaching the age of twenty-seven.

Now that she had a boyfriend, Qiqi felt more confident at work (grin). She picked a day and announced it to her colleagues. Pleased, her colleagues smiled with satisfaction when they heard the news. One of them even said, "Welcome! You are normal."

After that, just like everyone, after being in a relationship for a while, Qiqi's boyfriend invited her to meet his parents for the first time.

His parents are from ordinary families. They stay in a regular apartment. Their apartment isn't big either. Their living conditions are worlds apart compared to Qiqi's parents and relatives. Fortunately, his parents are relatively friendly, even though they are blunt in words. Qiqi knew that they were different from her parents. She chose not to comment or care about it. She thought she should be more tolerant since she is in a relationship with him. She isn't concerned with marrying into families with equal social statuses. In this age of science, it is sufficient if her boyfriend had a job and a decent degree. There is no need to be finicky.

Her boyfriend's parents were very satisfied with Qiqi. They even asked when they would get married.

However, her parents expressed their concerns as they were worried about their differences and if she wouldn't be able to get along with his family. Qiqi comforted her parents and said, "We wouldn't live together, so there wouldn't be a problem."

Moreover, Qiqi also said confidently, "Although I love my boyfriend, I won't lose my rationality. I will always maintain a clear mind when I'm with him."

Her parents agreed and didn't say anything anymore.

They got married and lived together.

The Winner in the
Hula Hoop Competition

Qiqi worked in the unit headquarters in the city. There were about two hundred employees in the headquarters alone while another few hundred worked in branches in other regions. They rarely see or know each other. The unit would often organize sports competitions to unite the employees and foster overall team spirit. The branches would select outstanding employees to compete in the finals, which would be held in the headquarters. Winners would be rewarded accordingly.

At that time, the headquarters would usually be lively. Many people from all the branches would get together as if old friends were reunited.

Qiqi didn't know anyone, so she could only listen to her colleagues. Her colleague explained to her as if she was telling a story, detailing Person X's resume, Person Y's background, etc. Smiling, Qiqi listened to it and thought life could be interesting yet complicated as well.

The unit organized a hula hoop competition. Qiqi wasn't very familiar with the hula hoop. Fortunately, the section had prepared leaflets in advance, and distributed to everyone in the unit, hoping that everyone could come and watch the game.

Qiqi looked at the contents on the leaflet. "Hula hoop was popular internationally in the 50s and 60s. As it is light and wouldn't take up much space, it quickly became a popular sport suitable for all ages. A skilled hula hoop player could train their abdomen and leg muscles, as well as strengthen their core muscles and improve the flexibility of their joints. In addition to being used as toys, the hula hoop is also used in acrobatic performances and competitions.

The hula hoops can be replaced by rhythmic gymnastics hoops as the competition requirements aren't strict. The hula hoop player needs to move around, so the hula hoop rotates around the body. The longer the player spins the hoop, the better the player is. This sport isn't intense. It is suitable for people of different ages. The hula hoop is both exciting and fun. Since its introduction in the 80s, it has grown widely popular across the country."

"Oh!" Qiqi finally understood. It was a new trend that was made popular overseas. No wonder she didn't know about it. To Qiqi, the people participating in the competition should have been practicing it usually. Qiqi's hobby is playing tennis. Tennis would need an open space outdoors, and it wasn't very convenient for the unit to organize tennis competitions. Meanwhile, hula hoop competitions could be held indoors.

Qiqi and her colleagues in the department went to watch the game together. It was held in a large hall in the unit. The hall was used for gatherings and competitions. Many commemorative events were held in the hall. The hall was enormous, and the stage was spacious. It could even fit a choir of six to seven rows during performances.

The competition started. At the beginning, a man and a woman appeared on the stage. They were the hosts for the competition. Qiqi recognized the female host. She was from another department. She had a fair complexion and a beautiful face, known by colleagues as the belle of the unit.

Meanwhile, Qiqi's attention was stolen when she laid her eyes on the male host. The man had a stylish haircut. He looked energetic in striped shirt and grey pants. He had a great body and a healthy complexion. Obviously, he had a better figure than ordinary people; no wonder he was chosen to be the host. He was total eye candy! Qiqi smiled and thought that the unit was smart enough to pick him as the host. Qiqi glanced at her colleague and asked, "The male host looks good. Is he from a good family?" Her colleague smiled and replied, "He's Zhang, and he's from one of the branches. We wouldn't be able to meet him normally." She paused and recalled before continuing, "No, he originated from a backward area. It's just that he loves fitness sports. He didn't have a good degree, and he only managed to get an associate degree." Qiqi seemed to understand her colleague's meaning. He was from a backward area, it meant he didn't have a good family background.

The competition was about to begin. A total of twenty contestants entered the stage one after another. Each person had a hula hoop. The competition rules were to spin the hula hoop continuously on the waist and maintain a leveled position. The hula hoop wasn't allowed to slide, tilt or fall. The winner would be the person who could spin the hoop persistently for a long time.

The colleagues who were watching the competition laughed when they heard the rules of the competition. Surely, the contestants would have amusing antics during the competition.

The game had started. The clock was ticking, and every contestant began to spin the hula hoop. It didn't matter how fast the contestant spun the hula hoop; the main goal was to spin consistently without falling. Qiqi knew, if the contestants tried to cut corners or lose their balance and spin too slowly, the hula hoop would fall because of the gravity. They would be violating the rules and eliminated from the game.

Turning and spinning, the contestants shook their bodies and raised their arms halfway up with confidence on their faces. The hula hoop spun steadily and quickly around their waist, and the crowd was cheering intently. Each contestant was selected to represent their branches, and they wouldn't fail easily. The crowd was excited and cheered enthusiastically, "Come on! Keep it up! Don't let the hula hoop fall!" The judges couldn't help but smile when they heard it.

Ten minutes passed, and most of the contestants were relatively steady. Fifteen minutes later, some contestant's hula hoop began to tilt. Some bright-eyed audience murmured, "Oh no, one of them wouldn't make it." Moments later, the hula hoop fell to the ground, and the contestant panted in exhaustion. The host then announced that the contestant was eliminated. Tension arose as the rest of the contestants continued to spin their hula hoops. The audience continued to scan the contestants on the stage. Qiqi found that one of the female contestants on the left side of the stage was spinning the hula hoop calmly. She was thin, yet she remained composed. As time progressed, multiple contestants were eliminated as their hula hoops fell to the ground. The host continued to eliminate the contestants as time went by. Some viewers were delighted, while others were glum.

Twenty minutes later, there were only three players left on the stage. They continued to spin their hula hoops steadily. It seemed that the final winners were these three contestants on the stage. Two out of the three contestants were visibly stronger and looked like they could persevere in the game. Meanwhile, the female contestant continued to spin the hula hoop calmly. Qiqi looked at her. She seemed to be very confident and had a look of victory. Qiqi wondered, "She's so thin, and hula hoop was a new sport. How could she play so skillfully?" Thirty minutes later, the competition was about to end, yet the three contestants continued to spin their hula hoops steadily. Finally, the judges announced that the three contestants on stage jointly won the first prize! Qiqi's colleague saw that Qiqi was staring at the female contestant the whole time.

She explained, "She's Yang, working in another branch. We won't get to see her normally."

Qiqi replied, "Oh, I see. Where is she working?"

"At the international airport. She's one of the few people with good degrees in the unit. She graduated from a prestigious university. It's the best university here."

Qiqi's colleague replied with a look of admiration. Qiqi was puzzled when she heard her colleague.

"A prestigious university?"

The NCEE is notoriously difficult, and it is obvious with the difficult test papers and the limited number of university admissions. Neither Qiqi nor her husband graduated from a prestigious university. It wouldn't be easy to enter a prestigious university.

Qiqi recalled her conversation with her high school teacher and asked, "What did she major in?"

"Foreign language. She took German." Qiqi's colleague replied. Qiqi continued, "I see, she majored in language."

Qiqi's colleague nodded. "Yeah, the unit values degrees from prestigious universities. I heard that she had a good degree, so the unit was going to promote and raise her salary."

Oh, Qiqi recalled the saying, "Those who excel in learning will be a good official." Society placed a lot of importance on a degree as it would bring many benefits. Qiqi smiled when she thought of it.

Her colleague nudged Qiqi with her elbow, "You're so sharp. Did you know the relationship between the man and woman you've just mentioned?"

Puzzled, Qiqi asked, "What's their relationship?" Her colleague replied, "They're husband and wife."

"Husband and wife?" This time, Qiqi was really surprised. It is a subversion of societal norms in terms of choosing a spouse.

The man only had an associate degree while the woman graduated from a prestigious university. How could they be husband and wife? Her colleague continued, "Yeah. People in the unit were talking about it and thought it was strange. The woman had such a good degree. Why did she pick a man who only had an associate degree? Even though he may be handsome, it couldn't replace the power of knowledge."

Qiqi nodded, agreeing with her colleague's statement. Back then, when she agreed to her husband's proposal, she also considered his level of education. In the age of science and technology, it is essential to consider a person's educational level instead of their appearance. It is superficial to judge a person by their appearance, and the same is true in marriage. Generally, women won't marry someone with a worse education unless there is a particular reason.

A few months passed. On the weekend, Qiqi suggested to her husband to go for a walk by the river since they hadn't been there for a long time. Her husband agreed.

Warm sun enveloped them as they strolled by the wide river. Qiqi and her husband felt bright and merry. They sat arm in arm in a higher terrain as they enjoyed the scenery in front of them. People walked past them with children in tow. Qiqi and her husband watched as the children ran happily on the field. They felt warm as they heard the children's giggly voices. Qiqi's husband muttered responsively,

"We'll also have children in the future." Qiqi nodded.

A couple was walking slowly, not too far away from them. Qiqi thought they looked familiar, so she looked at them again. It turned out to be the male host and the female contestant in the hula hoop competition! Qiqi's attention was fixed to them, but they never noticed her since they didn't know her. They were strolling leisurely and chatting intimately. Qiqi gazed at them intently as they moved around. As they slowly walked away, Qiqi thought something was missing. Oh yes, children! Qiqi recalled that her colleagues told her that the female contestant was three years older than her. She should have children by now.

Qiqi watched as they left. She recalled the gap between their education levels and told her husband about them. Then she asked, "If it were you, would you choose a woman with a higher educational level than yours?"

Her husband shook his head and replied, "It's okay if she's just a little bit better than me. But if her educational level is much better than mine, we cannot see eye to eye on many things. That might lead to fights. Then, I can't accept it." Qiqi nodded.

Her husband contemplated briefly before continuing, "A couple like them is rare and strange."

During a lunch break on a weekday, Qiqi told her colleague that she met the couple when she was taking a walk by the river that day. Her colleague nodded. "I heard that they were getting along well."

Qiqi asked, "Haven't they had children?"

Her colleague looked at her in admiration when she heard Qiqi, "You're on point! They don't have children. They are Dinks."

"Dinks?" Such concepts were strange and rare in this country. It was against the mainstream culture and social norms in this country. Qiqi widened her eyes in surprise.

Her colleague continued, "I heard that it was because she didn't want to have a child. The man had always liked the woman because she graduated from a prestigious university and had a good degree, so he relented."

Qiqi was dumbfounded and didn't know what to say. Her colleague looked at Qiqi and mediated, "Oh, leave them alone. There will always be people with peculiar behavior in the world. It's fine as long as we're normal."

The Metropolitan City

Time passed quickly and soon, it would be the twenty-first century. Everyone awaited the new era with anticipation.

The unit decided to hold a commodity test. Everyone would have to participate in it to usher in the arrival of the new century.

Qiqi loves knowledge and science very much. She thought that learning was a positive thing at work. The test was divided into two groups, 1 for men and another 1 for women. It was conducted formally in a college. The invigilators were the teachers in the college, and the test was formal.

The test included commodity subject and English. To Qiqi, the test wasn't difficult.

The results were out, and Qiqi won first place in the women's group. There was a lot of praise from Qiqi's colleagues, and Qiqi felt happy. She realized that her trips to the bookstore were beneficial, and it helped her to expand her knowledge and improve her understanding.

The unit management had a meeting and decided to send Qiqi and the men's group winner to the national training camp for training. For more than half a year, Qiqi received in-depth training in the national camp. The training content was cutting edge, and Qiqi's course was packed with activities. She attended lectures and practical classes, watched videos, had discussions in workshops, and wrote her thesis. It wasn't easy, but Qiqi felt more confident as she had improved a lot professionally.

Qiqi returned to the unit after the training. Before she managed to reunite with her colleagues again, she received a transfer notice from her superior. She would be transferred to a better role, a role in a metropolitan city to work in the Bureau. Her colleagues were envious, and some even bantered with her, "That's great! Why don't you take me along?"

Before she was transferred, Qiqi felt reluctant to leave the city and her colleagues, as she had a good relationship with them. Even though the metropolitan city was better, it was far and strange to Qiqi. Moreover, Qiqi wasn't familiar with the dialect in that city.

Concerned, her colleagues advised her, "The metropolitan city is packed with people, and it's complicated. You have to be careful." Qiqi nodded.

At home, Qiqi bid farewell to her husband. Her husband told her that he would also apply for a transfer, and they would be reunited in less than a year.

Before leaving, Qiqi went to the hospital for a body checkup. She realized that she was pregnant.

The new unit knew that Qiqi was pregnant after her arrival, so they gave her a lighter workload.

The metropolitan city is the most prosperous city in the country, and the population is more than 20 million. Known as the magical metropolis, the city looked modern, and the commercial streets were lined with shops.

Qiqi observed this city quietly. The high-rise buildings in this city are indeed denser than those in her hometown. The buildings are often built close to each other, and the space is very limited. Every inch of land is worth its weight in gold. Qiqi wanted to settle down and welcome her new life in this new city.

The house price is sky-high in this city. Qiqi and her husband were not financial enough to pay. Qiqi didn't want to take a loan because she would need to raise her baby, and it would cost a lot. Fortunately, her parents came to rescue, and the financial difficulty was solved. Qiqi heard that in the new unit, many colleagues took a mortgage as house prices were exorbitant. They had to work hard to repay their mortgages every month. Qiqi was thankful to God because she was born into a good family.

Half a year later, her husband's application for transfer was approved, and he was transferred to this city for work.

Qiqi gave birth to a baby girl. Although her husband was glad, he was a little disappointed as he longed for a boy. Qiqi herself is a woman, and she doesn't have any gender discrimination.

She persuaded her husband, "It's the 21st century now. In this age of science and technology, our daughter will be a valuable talent as long as we nurture her well."

Qiqi paused and continued in a firm tone, " It doesn't matter if the baby is a boy or a girl. I'll try my best to raise her well."

Qiqi's husband didn't comment further.

Qiqi felt that although modern society is developing rapidly, there are still prejudices brought about by traditions. She hoped that her daughter could purify the world and clear the dirt, just like the morning rain. So, she named her daughter "Clear".

Gradually, many colleagues in Qiqi's new workplace had children. After returning to work, Qiqi would often hear them gossiping about their family during their breaks. Sometimes, they would even whisper secretly in the local dialect. Qiqi couldn't understand them. Compared to her previous colleagues in her old workplace, she felt that her colleagues here seemed to like to chat about their children more than themselves.

Qiqi didn't like gossips. She came from a well-mannered family. She wasn't used to gossiping about her family or relatives. She knew that she was cultured, and her family was refined and exceptional. There is no need to talk about it. She didn't understand her colleagues. Why did they have so much to talk about?

Perhaps, the way people communicate here was different from

Qiqi's hometown, so the way the people behaved here was different as well.

In the community where Qiqi lived, many people were talking about money-related matters, be it discussions between neighbors or when people were waiting for the lift.

For instance, they would always ask, "How much do you earn in a month?"

"You don't have enough money? That won't do."

At the beginning, Qiqi couldn't get used to it. She thought it was rude and uncultured to talk about money in public. To Qiqi, the topic of money should be discussed at home during budgeting or discussions on living expenses. How could the topic of money be talked about so frequently during daily communication?

Qiqi thought that this city was too obsessed with money. Perhaps, it is due to the large population and the tension of sources of interests in the city. This is different from what Qiqi had thought before. She felt that people in metropolitan cities should be civilized and wealthy. She wouldn't have thought that people were so obsessed with money. She thought that such ambience was so weird.

Qiqi even thought, "Won't you turn shallow if you talk about money all day long?"

Slowly, Qiqi got used to it. She had to uphold her character and not follow the crowd, just like how she did during high school. Even with children, she wasn't like the other women, investing all her time and energy in her family. Despite her busy schedule at work and home, she managed to squeeze out some time to read and learn about natural science. She also had a special book in her room, which is not available to ordinary people in this country. It is a thick Bible, published and translated in the country's native language.

English is not official language in this country. There is no holiday during Christmas, and merchants will take the opportunity to promote their products aggressively during sales. But Qiqi wouldn't conform to the trend. Qiqi wouldn't go shopping, she would read the Bible during this time of the year. Qiqi thought that reading the Bible on the feast day is the most meaningful thing to do, and it is also the best way to commemorate the sage who is widely respected worldwide.

Besides praising righteous people, the stories in Bible also put forward many guiding precepts. This includes what not to do, not to be greedy etc. Qiqi thought that this is consistent with the purpose of law in modern society. Law in modern society emphasizes facts and evidence, while Bible preaches self-discipline in people.

Qiqi placed her hardcover Bible carefully in the transparent glass cabinet made of walnut so she could look at it whenever she wants. To Qiqi, the Bible is a gift to the world. There will be a pure space in one's heart that is isolated from worldly desires and interests such as money.

As the saying goes, "A gentleman's pursuit for money is bounded by ethics; he does not obtain it through dubious means."

"Life is something I desire, but there is something I desire more than life."

These two sayings mean that there is something more important in life than interests.

On the surface, although knowledge is transmitted through words, it is in fact explaining ideas and principles. The more knowledge one gains, the less one doubts and worries about the surrounding noises. They could better decide the direction of their lives and control their behavior. Qiqi believes that this is the confidence brought by knowledge, and it cannot be replaced by anything else in the world.

Qiqi's Migration

Qiqi's daughter, Clear, grew up quickly from a small fleshy and hairy fluff to a beautiful toddler. She started to have teeth and babbled. So lovely.

Clear's growth surprised Qiqi. She bought a camcorder to record time moments of her daughter's growth. Qiqi had also become the most important witness during her daughter's growth.

In this country where Qiqi resides, instructions and notices were issued by the central administration departments and subsequently transmitted to the states, provinces for them to implement and comply with the rules.

In the neighborhood where Qiqi lived, a "resident bulletin board" was set up in the most eye-catching place. Various paper notices were posted on the board, which are officially issued by official units. The content was about regulations made by the official organizations, and residents were notified to comply with these regulations.

Time flew by quickly. Soon, it was time for Qiqi's daughter to attend kindergarten. A formal paper notice was posted on the bulletin board. According to the relevant information that had been widely published, children were to be enrolled in nearby public kindergartens based on the address registered on their identity card. The name of kindergarten, address, telephone number, and time of registration were clearly written in the notice.

According to the requirements in the notice, Qiqi brought her daughter together with the relevant credentials to the kindergarten. There were a lot of parents in the kindergarten, and it was very lively. Many children lived nearby and knew each other. The parents knew each other as well. Qiqi met an acquaintance who lived in the same neighborhood. After a quick chat, Qiqi learned that she had sent her daughter here based on the notice. Her daughter was two years older than Clear, and she was in the senior class in kindergarten. Qiqi felt reassured after talking to her acquaintance. She trusted local educational organizations and handed her daughter over to the kindergarten teacher.

Qiqi knew that kindergarten is equivalent to pre-school education, where children mainly experience life in groups and gradually get used to learning in groups. This is preparation for formal schooling in the future.

There were a lot of children in the kindergarten, and there were many group activities. Clear was very concentrative in kindergarten. The teacher's feedback to Qiqi was that Clear had performed well in children. In the message book, Qiqi often saw the teacher's compliments for Clear.

There was also once where the kindergarten teacher took some photos of the year-end celebration to usher in the new year. It was a fashion performance where children were required to perform a catwalk on stage. After receiving the notice from the kindergarten, Qiqi considered it for a while and thought that while it is important and necessary to cultivate Clear's inner quality, she should also pay attention to her appearance as well.

So, Qiqi went to the children's counter in the mall. With Qiqi's refined taste, she carefully selected beautiful and appropriate outfits that wouldn't be too cold for winter. When she returned home, she dressed Clear elaborately from head to toe. Qiqi plaited her daughter's hair and put on white boots for her. She didn't stop for a moment and was clearly exhausted, but her hard work was paid off as Clear looked amazing in the new ensemble. In the fashion performance at the kindergarten, Clear looked amazingly beautiful and refined. Qiqi knew that it was the result of her hard work and a reflection of her rich talent. Qiqi hoped that her daughter's personality would turn out to be beautiful, just like how she looked during the fashion performance. She hoped that Clear would do her best once she decided to do something. Nevertheless, it should be something worth the effort.

As usual, Qiqi's colleagues talked about their children during breaks in excitement. Qiqi didn't participate in the discussions, but she heard them talking about enrolling in hobby classes. Qiqi couldn't agree with the idea of arranging children to enroll in hobby classes since young. To Qiqi, a child's growth is a brand-new stage of life. Parents should observe their children and understand their strengths. Kids would decide their interests for themselves, as parents should provide financial support for their children.

Qiqi wasn't a tiger parent, and she didn't have the command style commonly seen in this country. She thought that parents should maintain friendly relationships with their children. They could encourage kids with their own excellence.

Qiqi observed her new colleagues. But after all, she didn't understand their dialect and didn't want to join them as well. Qiqi also didn't tell them about her family background. She didn't want to do that because such behavior wasn't in line with Qiqi's good upbringing. She didn't want to rely on the glory of her family to elevate her position. She believed that everyone had their value, and everyone should be hardworking. Qiqi knew she was excellent and then that was enough.

Among the department colleagues, one of female colleagues attracted Qiqi's attention. She was relatively short. Qiqi's height was 1.6 meters, and it is considered medium height for women. Qiqi smiled as her new colleague still couldn't reach her height despite wearing high heels.

"How could she be so short?" Qiqi thought.

Qiqi once read a book that explored the correlation between height and brainpower. In addition to genetic factors, shorter people have better brainpower than others. That is because they spend a lot of energy in thinking, and from a medical point of view, this inhibits the development of other parts of the body.

The female colleague, named Zhu, is younger than Qiqi but looks older than her. Her face is peppered with freckles, and it left an unpleasant impression on people in terms of appearance. What was strange to Qiqi was that Colleague Zhu seemed to feel good about herself all day long. She was always self-centered about herself. She had an important position at work to modify the data information. Qiqi knew that it was an important position as she had the authority to change or delete the information other colleagues had confirmed. Qiqi couldn't help but learn about Colleague Zhu from other colleagues.

Her colleague replied, "She's a local. She has deep relationships here and is very close to some of leaderships in the unit. We can't compare to her. Plus, she had a degree from a regular university. So, although she didn't have a lot of experience, the department gave her an important role."

"Oh, I see." Qiqi somewhat understood. It seemed that Colleague Zhu was good at interpersonal relations. Then she pondered before asking, "What's her major?"

"It's foreign language."

Confused, Qiqi thought, "How could her major be foreign language?"

Generally, her major would allow her to speak with foreigners, and she should be assigned to work in port location, such as Qiqi's hometown. Qiqi could recall that the contestant who won the hula hoop competition was also assigned to work in locations such as the international airport, where there needed a lot of oral communications with foreigners.

Qiqi's colleague saw through her queries and said, "I'm not too sure about her degree since she rarely talks about it.

"Why don't we ask her?" She spoke. Qiqi nodded.

The two of them acted casually. They went to Colleague Zhu's desk and asked politely, "Teacher Zhu (a polite appellation), I heard that you had a decent degree, and we envy you. You majored in foreign language, right? What minor foreign language is it?" Colleague Zhu was still grinning a while ago. The next moment, her face immediately became serious when she heard them. She kept quiet, and there was an awkward tension in the air. Qiqi and her colleague were confused and wondered what had gone wrong. Did something strange happen? After some time, Qiqi's colleague grew anxious and nudged Colleague Zhu, "Hey, what minor foreign language did you learn?" Qiqi clearly saw Colleague Zhu's reluctance and discomposure before she heard her short reply in a low voice, "French."

Qiqi thought to herself, "Having a degree from a formal university is kind of brilliance. Why did Colleague Zhu seem so reluctant to mention it? "

In this metropolitan city, the Commodity Management Bureau had a relatively heavy workload, and there are more companies that came to submit their orders compared to Qiqi's hometown. Every day, Qiqi's current department would receive multiple submissions or inquiries from companies.

When they got to know each other closely, Qiqi could see that Colleague Zhu often speaks vulgarly in her day-to-day life. This added to Qiqi's doubts. Colleague Zhu didn't seem like a proper undergraduate who possessed higher educational level but rather a boorish and uncultured woman on the streets. Colleague Zhu's role was to handle information modification. For a while, Qiqi was seated very close to her, and she could hear her style of speech closely face to face. It was something one should experience in person, as it was an eye-opening behavior.

During working hours, Qiqi often heard Colleague Zhu cast some wild words. She once rebuked a man who came to consult her and ridiculed a woman's makeup who came to hand in some documents.

Qiqi was surprised to hear such uncivilized words. She worked for many years, visited the Commodity Management Bureau in other cities, and was sent to the national training camp for an advance. She had never encountered someone who would speak so egoistically during the working time. Moreover, she is a woman, yet her words are of low quality. It was obvious that she had a bad upbringing and lacked civilization.

Qiqi thought that it was unbearable to get along with people like Colleague Zhu. Later, when the department adjusted the seating arrangement for staff, Qiqi requested to be seated further away. That is because Qiqi had a good upbringing since young. Her mind is pure and unpolluted with vulgar thoughts. Now that she had met such a crude people in her work and had to get along with her, she just wanted to stay away from these low-level people as it was the best way to maintain her purity.

When she was resting at home, Qiqi quietly sorted out her thoughts calmly. She recalled the moments from the time she first started work in her hometown to the time when she was transferred to this city for work. She had encountered so many odd people and thought that the people in the metropolitan city were not as civilized and courteous as reported on TV. The residents, especially those who can speak in dialect, were pretentious and mighty, thinking that they were more superior to others. Qiqi recalled her mother and colleague's advice when she left her hometown, advising her to be careful as there are all sorts of people in the city, and city people are more complicated.

Qiqi turned her head and looked at the Bible inside the glass cabinet. The Bible laid there, calm and peaceful. The bright sun shone in from the window and penetrated through the glass cabinet. The gentle light illuminated the Bible, radiating a soothing and lasting warmth. Qiqi couldn't help but pray in her heart.

CHAPTER EIGHT

The Elementary and Middle School

Time flew past, and Clear was at the age to enroll in elementary school and about to enter the school system.

Like kindergarten, a formal notice was posted on the residents' bulletin board, informing children with citizenship to enroll in a designated public elementary school nearby. The elementary public school's name, address, and phone number were clearly announced on the bulletin board.

Qiqi was delighted. It was a momentous event in her daughter's life as she was about to enroll officially in school. Qiqi embarked on a tighter schedule. Every day, she would send her daughter to school and go to work. After Qiqi's husband picked up their daughter in the afternoon, they would gather and have dinner at night. After that, Qiqi would check her daughter's homework as well as other aspects in school.

Clear was very disciplined. In school, she would focus on class, abide by school rules, and not get into fights with her classmates. She would consistently score above 90 in every test. Qiqi was pleased that her daughter had been so disciplined since young. She would be able to maintain her discipline in the future.

Clear had excellent grades. Slowly, her classmates requested to do their homework with Clear after school. They usually followed her back home together. They only returned to their own home after finishing their homework.

Qiqi thought it was strange, so she asked her daughter, "Why did they come to our house to do homework with you?" "That's because they couldn't solve the problems. Since they need to keep asking me, they came home together with me," her daughter replied.

"Oh, I see." Qiqi stopped asking.

She was moved, she cherished the children. Who wouldn't want to do well in school? Even at such a young age, Clear's classmates knew the importance of studying and chose to learn from others after school. It was arrangement from educational organizations arranging such heavy courses and challenging tests, causing immense pressure for the students.

The emotion lingered in Qiqi's heart for a long time. She glanced at the date on the calendar and realized that it was her daughter's birthday soon. Qiqi decided to take this opportunity to organize a birthday party and gather her daughter's classmates together for a wonderful time together. Childhood should be filled with happiness.

Kids shouldn't be studying so hard and become machines under stress. The birthday was coming, and the party was arranged for a weekend. Qiqi asked her daughter to write down the names of the classmates she had invited. Then she prepared the invitation card in advance to invite the children over to the birthday party, specifically stating that there was no need to prepare gifts.

On that day, Qiqi and her husband's plan was to let the children to light candles and eat the birthday cake to celebrate before going to a restaurant during lunchtime for a good meal.

Clear was beautifully dressed. With a bow in her hair, she was the star of the party. When it was time, there was a knock at the door, and her classmates came in one after another joyfully while wishing "Happy Birthday" to her. They also brought out gifts simultaneously and passed the gift to Clear shyly with blushed faces. Every one of them prepared gifts. Qiqi was very surprised as she had never expected it since she had stated in the invitation that there was no need to prepare a gift. How sweet the children were!

"Have all your classmates arrived? Can we start the party? Blow the candles and cut the cake?" Qiqi asked Clear.

She replied, "Not, not yet. Classmate Lu hasn't arrived." Qiqi continued, "Is it a boy or a girl?"

"It's a boy," She replied. "Alright, then let's wait for him."

Not long after, Qiqi's house phone rang. It was a call from Classmate Lu's parents, informing them that their son would be late as he had tuition class. They also told Qiqi that they should start the party and not wait for him.

"Alright then, let's get started!"

Qiqi brought out the double-layered birthday cake and lighted the candles. They took a few pictures with the cake since it looked beautiful. Clear's classmates looked adorable as they stared at the double-layered cake with swaying candlelight. The party started, and Clear made a wish and blew the candles. Finally, it was time to cut the cake.

It was more difficult to cut a double-layered cake. Fortunately, Qiqi's husband helped to cut it into small pieces and placed it on the plates. The kids couldn't wait to eat it. Qiqi prepared some fruits and drinks, as well as some black tea. The kids ate happily. Some even had some cream on their mouths and looked like a cartoon character. Qiqi burst into a giggle as she watched them on the side. One of the children even said excitedly, "I'll have a birthday party next time! I'll invite everyone to the party!"

Qiqi's husband took out the camera and recorded the rare and fun times the children had during the party. Then he used a video cable to connect it to the TV and adjust the settings. The TV played the video he had just recorded. The children were amazed, "Hey! We're on TV! Look! We're on TV!" Qiqi and her husband smiled with delight.

"Happy times and happy children. This is the joy and happiness you should have."

Qiqi thought as she prayed for them silently in her heart. "Classmate Lu hasn't arrived. What should we do?"

They couldn't be late since they had made a reservation in the restaurant.

It was time to go. Everyone was waiting anxiously at the gates of the community for his arrival. Finally, he arrived. A parent zoomed past quickly in an electric bike. The bike screeched to a stop, and Classmate Lu appeared in the back seat. "He's here!" Qiqi looked and was shocked.

"Why is he so short? He was significantly shorter than other children of his age."

She found that the child wasn't at the height of an elementary school student but the height of toddlers in kindergarten.

Qiqi asked her daughter quietly, "Is this your classmate? Why haven't I seen him before?"

"Oh, he had never been to our house. He has good grades, and we usually discuss difficult problems together at school, so I invited him," Clear replied.

"Good grades? She said that he had good grades.

"Doesn't Clear have good grades as well?" Qiqi thought, shocked to hear her daughter's praise.

Confused, Qiqi asked quietly, "What do you mean?"

Qiqi's daughter saw through her mother's doubts. She nodded, affirming her suspicions, and said, "He had good grades and always scored 95 and above in tests. He's one of the rare students in my class that has better grades than me."

"I see." Qiqi replied. She went into contemplation.

"He scores 95 and above in every test? A full mark is only 100 test points! This is unusual. Even though he may had attended tuition during weekends, it wouldn't be possible to achieve such excellent results," Qiqi thought.

It could only be he had spent too much time and energy on studying. Just like now, he couldn't even eat the cake. He missed the birthday party and wasn't recorded in the video. He didn't even manage to watch the birthday party video.

Qiqi felt sad. She knew that all the sacrifices made were for the dreaded NCEE. It was for the grades and test scores that the child had missed the fun during childhood. What a pity!

She lifted her head and looked at Classmate Lu again.

"Oh, his height! He's shorter than average compared to his classmates! It was so glaringly obvious!"

Qiqi recalled the physiology book she had previously read. The book put forward a theory: Aside from the genetic factors, short people often have better brainpower compared to regular people. It was because they spent more energy thinking. From a scientific perspective, it would inhibit the growth and development of the other parts of the body.

Deep inside, Qiqi felt unwell. She would never expect that her daughter's birthday party would reflect the theory put forward in the book—poor children, drowning themselves in practice questions and training so early for the NCEE.

Since then, Qiqi had been secretly worrying about her daughter's health.

As time flew by, Qiqi's daughter graduated from elementary school and would go to junior middle school. This country implements a 9-year compulsory education system, i.e., five years of elementary school and four years of junior middle school. Based on admission information that had been widely publicized to the public, students would need to enroll in the nearby public schools according to the address on their ID. In other words, the local educational organizations would assign public schools to students. If the student abandoned the designed public school, he could choose private school.

Qiqi was extremely concerned about this matter and had been waiting for the announcement on the community bulletin board. It was a crucial stage because entering middle school meant entering the secondary school stage, and that would lead to the NCEE. Which middle school would Clear be assigned to? She waited anxiously, but there was no notice or announcement coming.

Puzzled, Qiqi thought, "Why didn't the local educational organizations issue paper notice? There wasn't any notice on the community bulletin board."

After days of frustration, Clear finally came back and told her, "Our elementary school announced that the admissions to junior middle school would be decided by drawing lots. The middle school will send people to each elementary school to draw lots based on student numbers. Whoever is drawn will go to whichever school that was selected."

"Oh, looks like the enrollment in junior middle school is different from elementary school," Qiqi muttered. She thought the arrangement was weird. She had heard from people in the community that some private schools outside were good, but it was too far away, and her daughter was too young. She chose to trust local educational organizations and went ahead with the arrangement.

Clear came back and told Qiqi about the process during the selection. There were a few middle schools nearby that came to draw lots. Among them, there was a reputable middle school, but the slots were limited. There were only two slots for her class, and all students were eager to be selected. They hoped that they would be drawn; at the same time, they wanted to see who would become the chosen one. Since only two slots were available, only two students would be selected. The first lot was drawn, and it was Clear's student number. She was selected!

Qiqi was delighted when she heard Clear said. To Qiqi, it was God's will that her daughter was selected. It was also God's reward for their trust in the national education system.

Clear embarked on her studies in middle school. Every morning, Qiqi would accompany her daughter to school, and they would pass by the bus stop on the way. At the bus stop, she often saw some students, seemingly the same age as Clear. Qiqi observed them and realized that they still had baby faces, yet they carried heavy schoolbags on them.

Some students had no schoolbags; they placed their books in a small suitcase and dragged them forward.

"The books and school supplies should be even heavier inside," Qiqi thought. That was why they had to use a suitcase instead of a school bag, and Qiqi couldn't bear to look at them anymore.

Sensible and disciplined, Clear studied hard as always. But Qiqi was a little worried that Clear's health would be affected due to long hours of studying. She often reminded her daughter to have enough rest, not to get too tired, and not hurt health. Clear nodded but still, she started to wear glasses due to long hours of study. Qiqi was gloomy to see her wearing glasses at such a young age.

The semester examination passed, and Clear's school informed the parents that a parent meeting would be held. Qiqi attended it. When Qiqi arrived at the school, she saw the welcome board in the entrance hall. Besides the eye-catching painted slogan: "Welcome to the parents meeting," a list of outstanding students was posted next to it, with the aim to boost students' morale.

Qiqi was a little embarrassed to see Clear's name listed on the board. She blushed and entered the classroom quietly.

The school was known for its foreign language, especially English. Due to that, the school had partnered with various foreign schools, and there were foreign teacher exchanges. Qiqi was curious; she wanted to know the secret the school could maintain the students' English ability.

Each subject's teachers appeared in turn. They went into the classroom and explained their class and the students' academic performance. Finally, the English teacher arrived. When she appeared on stage, she had a formidable aura. Other teachers were calm and polite in interactions while the English teacher was special. Her tone was condescending, as if she was disciplining the parents. Qiqi held her smile as she knew that it was how things were in this country. As a developing country in the far east, the advancement of science and economy in this country were only average while the English language countries were obviously more advanced in terms of international standards. Naturally, English teachers were prouder.

Qiqi heard the English teacher's request for parents to urge their children to read the English course materials for 15 times. According to her, that was a satisfactory learning outcome. Qiqi thought that the request was heavy burden. The purpose of learning is to understand and master the knowledge. Reading the course materials up to 15 times repeatedly would only waste the students' energy and exhaust them. Qiqi now understood why her daughter was nearsighted; it was because the schoolwork was too heavy.

At one time, Clear was unwell and fell ill. The hospital issued a medical certificate, and she was told to rest for a period. After resting for a few days, Clear wanted to go back to school again. Qiqi disagreed, but Clear wanted to take the monthly test as her school had tests every month. Qiqi disapproved; she thought that Clear should stay at home and rest since it was only a monthly test. Plus, she had notified the school with a medical certificate. But Clear insisted on going to school; she also said something that Qiqi remembered for a long time, "If I don't take the test, my class's average score will drop."

Clear had always been excellent in her studies, especially in science and mathematics. She remained studious even when facing difficult and strange problems. Qiqi knew the amount of effort and energy Clear devoted and commended her for enduring hardships. However, at the same time, she sympathized to see Clear studying so hard.

The four years of education in junior middle school were soon over. Qiqi knew that the legal education mandated by the country was ending soon. It was five years of elementary school education and four years of junior middle school education. Clear completed her mandatory education as stipulated by local educational organizations.

After middle school, students would enter high school in the next stage of education. A standardized examination across the city would be held. There were four excellent high schools, all of which were commonly known as the "Four Safes" in public. With these outstanding high schools, students would have a higher chance of getting into a prestigious university during the NCEE. Hence, many students and their parents were desperate to be admitted to these schools.

Clear went to the entrance examination calmly without asking her parents to accompany her.

She managed to obtain excellent results in the examination. She was admitted to the city's best science high school with top score.

CHAPTER NINE

The High School and the National College Entrance Examination

In the four top high schools, all the students who passed the examination were top students. Qiqi couldn't help but feel emotional when she looked at her daughter's thin body and realized that Clear had become a top student too. The NCEE was difficult, and many things could happen during the examination. Qiqi decided that no matter what Clear's college entrance examination results were in the future, she wouldn't blame Clear because Clear had proved that she was an outstanding student.

Not long after entering the school, the school issued a notice after a series of tests, hoping that students would sign up for the International Olympiad. Clear came home and asked Qiqi if she should participate in the competition. Qiqi found it strange as Clear had just started her first year of high school. Why should she prepare for the competition instead of focusing on her studies? Clear explained that the school had arrangements for the Olympiad class. First-year high school students would complete all the courses in high school rapidly so they could prepare for the Olympiad in their second year of high school. Students would then immerse themselves in the sea of practice questions, and outstanding students would be selected to represent in the Olympiad. If the student managed to win awards in the international competition such as gold or silver medal, the student would receive recommendation to university, which means that they would be recommended and admitted directly to university in relevant majors without having to take the NCEE. If there were students who were unwilling to be recommended and still wanted to take the NCEE, they would receive an extra 20-points during the NCEE according to the educational policy. Then, they would take the NCEE together with regular students in the third year of high school.

Shocked, Qiqi frowned after she heard about it. To Qiqi, the school was not doing things right. Such an arrangement wouldn't only fill up the student's schedules, but it would also overload them with activities. Wouldn't the students be exhausted with the packed schedule? How could the school force the students to study so hard for the Olympiad?

"Let the physically strong boys participate in the Olympiad then," Qiqi said. She didn't allow her daughter to participate in it. However, Clear came back and told her that according to the teacher, she needed a reason not to participate in it.

Qiqi sighed and told Clear, "Alright, why don't we delay your participation? You can observe the students who participated in the

Olympiad class. If you think they are fine, you can participate then."

After some time, Clear came home. She nodded to Qiqi and decided not to participate in the Olympiad class anymore as the students who participated in the class seemed to be abnormal. They would even tilt their head and seemed to be constantly thinking problems even when they walked. Some students even withdrew from the class, citing that it was too tiring.

Qiqi nodded and declared to her daughter, "No matter how beneficial or tempting things are, we won't do things that will hurt our health."

The workload in high school was horrifying. Clear had her own room, and Qiqi saw that there were more and more reference books piling up in the room, filling up the existing four-story bookcase. The books were piled up on other furniture such as on the cabinet, table, and everywhere else. The books were selection of difficult problems, and they were large. They were thick and heavy, many of them were the size of A4 paper. There were also many dictionaries that Qiqi couldn't even hold with one hand as it was too heavy. On the eve of the NCEE, the books in Clear's room had piled up to a terrifying level. Everywhere were books! The books were not only stacked on the table and the cabinets in the room but also on the bed and the wooden floor in the room. The room seemed like sea with books, and books piled up everywhere like hills, covering the entire room. If someone wanted to enter the room, they would have to lift their feet, lean sideways, and carefully walk through it. Qiqi was shocked by the horrifying scene and wanted to tidy up her daughter's room. Clear stopped her, "Don't touch them! I've categorized them, and I want to read them!"

Qiqi was heartbroken. She couldn't imagine how Clear endured such tremendous hardships and competed with tens of thousands or even hundreds of thousands of people to enter university. The six subjects in the NCEE were notoriously difficult, complex, and unpredictable. It was as though the subjects were fierce tigers, ready to threaten the future and destiny of the students. Meanwhile, Clear had to find weapons to fight and overcome these tigers among books!

Clear's diligence and hard work had produced excellent results. She got excellent scores in mathematics and physics. She was among the excellent in the class, especially in physics. In the third year of high school, she often got Grade A+ in physics. Qiqi looked at Clear's student transcript with admiration. She knew that getting full marks in physics in the best science high school was almost impossible for ordinary students. Clear was indeed a talent. The school had also suggested Clear to apply for Jinghua University.

Although Qiqi was delighted, she was worried as her daughter was thin and her face grew paler and paler. Would her diligence affect her health?

Clear had to take six subjects in total for the NCEE. This included Language, Mathematics, English, Physics/Chemistry, Biology, and Geography. She had to do in-depth revisions for all the subjects. In addition to understanding the subjects, memorizing the facts, reading, and reciting the course materials, she also needed to do a lot of difficult problems from question banks, which contained various complicated and strange problems that Clear had never seen before. She had to understand and solve the problems. Daytime was just not enough, and Clear had to devote her time at night to study as well. Every day, she studied until late at night, and became the last person in the family to fall asleep. Clear's frail body couldn't withstand the intense workload around the clock. Finally, she fainted at school and was sent to the school infirmary. The school doctor was worried. He called Qiqi to explain the situation and reminded Clear to rest more. Qiqi took her daughter home and asked Clear to stop studying and lie down to rest. Clear slept for three nights in a row. When she got better, she got up and went out, wanting to rush to school to attend class as she was afraid that she would be left behind in her studies. Qiqi couldn't stop her daughter from leaving. As Qiqi watched Clear leaving to school in a hurry, she couldn't help but question the intention of the way used by the education department.

Qiqi felt that in the eyes of the education department, most students at regular schools are not important people, and it is up to the education department to decide their future. The reality in society is clear: People must have a job if they want a living income, and job opportunities are often obtained only by having a degree. The education department rules over higher education throughout the country. In other words, they can control people's predictable social fate.

Qiqi took the NCEE before and understood the pain caused by the NCEE: **The student who is preparing for the NCEE not only needs to study hard to improve himself but also to suppress other students' excellence. Only in this case can he improve his ranking and qualify for university admission.** The NCEE is stained with the students' sweat, tears, and it is full of hardship and torment. In other words, the education department does not cherish most students at least. So, they use ruthless unified examination to select students by exact score ranking.

Such a way is widely promoted by the education department in this country and is strongly disseminated as the exemplary and fair selection method. Through official publicity, this propaganda has been spreading to thousands of households and is deeply rooted in people's minds. The method is regarded by the public as the fair route to enter university.

The NCEE was approaching, and it was a major event in Clear's life. The examination would take three days in total. Qiqi had decided that she would ask leave on working and accompany her daughter. A nationwide examination is often eventful and a crucial period in this country. Media would focus on reporting about the NCEE, and parents would escort students to boost their morale. Qiqi felt that even if Clear didn't want her company, she should fulfill her responsibility and wait for her at home. At the same time, she wanted to feel the intense atmosphere from the NCEE.

Qiqi submitted her leave request to the unit. Her colleagues were concerned when they heard that Qiqi's daughter would take the NCEE. A few of them came over to enquire on her, and they discussed each other. Everyone knew that sooner or later; their children would also have to take the NCEE.

The arrangement of the NCEE was strict. The examination was not set in Clear's school, as another school was selected as the examination venue instead. Admission cards were issued to the students. The admission card contained the picture and details of the student. The invigilator would check the admission card and verify the student's identity before allowing them to take the examination. Qiqi accompanied Clear and went to familiarize herself with the examination venue, and they planned out the time of arrival in advance.

Clear was a little nervous. After all, it was a critical moment in her life, and there was no room for mistakes. Otherwise, there would be serious consequences and lifelong impacts. Qiqi patted her daughter's shoulders and advised her, "Relax, don't be nervous, and do your best in the examination. Don't consider anything else."

Clear asked Qiqi not to accompany her to the examination in case she didn't do well in the first subject examination as Qiqi would ask about the exam, affecting her mood for the next subject examination. Qiqi pondered and thought that it made sense, so she made necessary arrangements and agreed to wait at home not to affect Clear to the greatest extent.

It was examination day, and the NCEE officially started. Clear took the exam in the examination hall while Qiqi waited at home quietly. Qiqi wasn't too nervous about the examination. She knew how excellent her daughter was, and she believed that even if there were some mistakes, it wouldn't be too bad. Nevertheless, she still felt uneasy. After all, the examination hall was a battlefield without gunpowder, and there were bound to be variables. Clear had worked so hard, studied for more than ten years relentlessly day and night, and did countless hard questions for the NCEE. In this country, people's social status is usually determined by the NCEE. Society and employers value the importance and weight of the NCEE. Who wouldn't give their all in the NCEE? Who wouldn't be nervous? Thousands of households worry about their children during the NCEE, sharing the anguish and tension during the uncertain time.

After the examination was over, Clear returned home, closed her room door, and started to weep sorrowfully. Qiqi knew that something must have gone wrong, so she knocked on her daughter's room. She could hear Clear sobbing and whimpering.

She muttered incoherently and intermittently, "I didn't do well… didn't… do… well… Language and biology" Qiqi's mind went blank, and she stunned. She managed to calm down after a while and asked eagerly, "What happened?" Clear sobbed and replied, "The essay theme was difficult, and the biology paper had a lot of medical questions that I had never seen before."

Clear continued to cry at home for several days in a row and didn't eat much. Qiqi also heard the social talk, people talked about that this year's exam questions were more difficult than last year. They didn't know why either.

There were no words to express Qiqi's grief and anger.

Colleague Zhu's Pride

A dozen or twenty days passed. Both Qiqi and her daughter were quiet, and there was a heavy silence at home. Meanwhile, Clear went to school for a few days and remained silent after returning home.

Doom and gloom surrounded the family until one day, Qiqi came home from work and saw a letter placed strategically on the table. She looked at the title. It was an admission letter! She quickly picked it up and read the content carefully. It was an admission letter from a top university that was ranked 4th in the country. Although Clear had lost her chance to enter the best university in the country, i.e., Jinghua University, gaining admission to this university wasn't bad either. Moreover, it was the alma mater of the late Dr. Qian, a famous expert from the California Institute of Technology. In other words, Clear would become an alumna of this university together with Dr. Qian. Qiqi was overjoyed! She held the admission letter up high with both hands to appreciate it. It was the proof of more than ten years of turmoil, sweat, and tears, as well as countless days and nights of hard work!

Qiqi congratulated Clear. She was still in a state of shock. She muttered something, seemingly to comfort herself and her mother. "Thank god I didn't completely fail in the exam." Qiqi nodded.

After entering her own room, Qiqi closed the door and wiped her wet eyes. Every student's parent must have waited for this moment in anticipation. Although the university wasn't the best, it was still considered good news. This wasn't an easy feat. Just like the Olympic Games, medal winners would often shed tears because they were aware of how much sacrifice they made for that moment!

The NCEE results were released. The media broadcasted a series of interviews and reports regarding the NCEE. There were joys and sorrows in each household. Those who won the exam congratulated each other, and the whole family basked in joy. Those who failed the exam and lost their chance to get into a university were down in the dumps. Some students didn't manage to score good results and they decided to retake the examination the next year to qualify for a prestigious university. Qiqi was strongly affected by that news and understood how prestigious it was for her daughter to qualify into the 4th excellent university in the country as regular students wouldn't be able to achieve it.

Qiqi's colleagues took the initiative to ask her when they saw her in the unit. "Did your daughter do well in the examination? Which university was she admitted to?"

First, Qiqi tried to be modest and told them that her daughter didn't do very well in the examination before telling them the university she got into. Her colleagues were thrilled and praised, "That's great! It's tough to pass the examination. Your daughter is excellent!"

The good news spread like wildfire in the unit. During lunch, even colleagues from other departments came over to congratulate Qiqi. They asked for her advice on the learning methods that could make their children excel in their studies. Qiqi told them how her daughter studied and preached about the importance of self-discipline, being hardworking, and doing more problems. Many colleagues were very encouraged by Qiqi. One of them even said, "You're an excellent mother, and you're our role model!" Qiqi smiled; she didn't mean to brag. She told them because her colleagues were eager to know the secret behind her daughter's success.

Qiqi had always made no proclamation about her family's excellence to others. She knew that she came from a knowledgeable family, and she didn't need to tell anyone to gain a sense of superiority. The fact that the 4th excellent university had accepted her daughter was only considered as a moderately excellent event in her family. It wasn't the best degree. Where was the best degree? Thinking of this, Qiqi smiled silently in her heart. The best degree was from Jinghua University and had always been stored by Qiqi. It was a testament to Qiqi's excellence. It was because of her excellence that the owner of the degree fell in love with her and adored her.

During lunchtime, Qiqi drank some water in the pantry to moisten her throat as she was a little tired from all the talking with her colleagues just now. There was no one in the pantry, and it was quiet.

At this time, the "distant" Colleague Zhu came in. The reason Qiqi referred to her as "distant" was because she hadn't had any contact with her for a long time.

Qiqi greeted her by nodding. Colleague Zhu was probably huffish when she saw that Qiqi was surrounded and praised by her colleagues during lunchtime. Her face was gloomy, and she didn't respond to Qiqi's greeting. Her tone was bossy, and she simply blurted something without any proof. "Are there any additional bonus points added to your daughter's score in the NCEE?" Qiqi looked at Colleague Zhu. It was obvious that she wanted to compete with Qiqi. Qiqi thought it was very strange, so she posed a question back to her. "What are you talking about? What bonus points? No, there aren't any bonus points added to her score." Colleague Zhu's face immediately paled, and she left the pantry, speechless and resentful.

Qiqi was baffled by her question. Qiqi and her family had always been upright and had exemplary personality. They would never engage in conniving and opportunistic acts. Qiqi knew that, in society, some students rely on competition awards to gain bonus points, so they have advantages in the NCEE. That was one reason why her daughter's high school valued the Olympiad and asked the students to train for it.

The NCEE is held in June, and the university admission is in July. Time flew, and six months had passed. It was the end of the year, and soon, a new year would start. Clear had also studied in the same university as Dr. Qian for half a year. When she returned home, she told Qiqi that the lecturers often talked about the expert Qian in the university. They even kept the physics paper he did in the past, in which he scored 96 marks. Qiqi was glad when she heard about it. Dr. Qian was the best physics expert in this country, and his life experience was even made into a movie. He was highly respected and admired by the people. It suddenly occurred to Qiqi. "Why didn't Dr. Qian get into the best university in the country?" Oh, the competition must be fierce, and he didn't have the opportunity to enter that university. Once again, Qiqi sighed at the power of unified examination.

It was the first month of the new year. In the department, Qiqi was disturbed by Colleague Zhu's loud voice in recent days. There was a time when Qiqi left her seat and walked toward Colleague Zhu's seat, wanting to know if something had happened over there. Several colleagues were muttering around Colleague Zhu. They immediately stopped talking and kept quiet when they saw Qiqi. After glancing around, Qiqi fixed her eyes on Colleague Zhu, only to see that she had an uncontrollable triumphant expression on her face. It was obvious that she was extremely proud. Colleague Zhu turned away and restrained her emotions after she saw Qiqi. Sensitive, Qiqi knew that something had happened, and it was related to herself. Qiqi thought it was strange. Colleague Zhu was a local in this metropolitan city. She had a solid foundation and had good relationships with the locals. Qiqi had always kept her distance from Colleague Zhu. What matters could be related to Qiqi? Qiqi asked, "What happened?" A colleague in the group quickly replied, "Nothing, we're just chatting."

Time seemed to move quickly. Soon, it was time for the NCEE again. The TV and media had been reporting about the NCEE, and Qiqi's colleagues were also talking about it in accordance with current affairs. Qiqi saw several colleagues walking towards Colleague Zhu's seat while saying, "Colleague Zhu was great! Her daughter was excellent!" Qiqi was attentive and realized that they were talking about the NCEE since the examination was ongoing. Qiqi listened to their conversations, and one of the colleagues who was closed to Colleague Zhu said, "Colleague Zhu's daughter was admitted to Yanjing University six months ago. It was the 2nd excellent university in our country, and she didn't need to take the NCEE!" Qiqi was stunned when she heard it.

Qiqi couldn't believe it; she thought she should ask Colleague Zhu directly to avoid any misunderstandings. So, she went to Colleague Zhu's place and asked politely, "Mrs. Zhu, has your daughter passed the NCEE?" Since Colleague Zhu could no longer keep it a secret, she decided to spill the beans. She side-eyed Qiqi, straightened her back arrogantly, and shook her head haughtily, "My daughter doesn't need to take the NCEE; she was recommended to university and now she has been resting for half a year!"

Colleague Zhu's usual speech and behavior, combined with her arrogance and crass attitude, left a bad impression on Qiqi. Qiqi couldn't believe that someone like Colleague Zhu would raise good children. Anyone who is good at learning will spend a lot of time and energy on learning. In the learning stage, the student would usually be in a calm and quiet state, just like Qiqi's daughter, who had full marks in Physics. It wasn't easy to have the great score in Physics, and the student would need to spend a lot of time studying, doing problems, and thinking. All of this would require time and peaceful environment. Colleague Zhu spoke constantly, and her speech was crude and vulgar. Qiqi found it hard to believe that such a person would have an outstanding daughter.

A student recommended for admission meant that the student would be admitted to university without taking the NCEE. This is a special treatment with great benefits. The types of recommendations widely known in the public are Olympiad students, sports medalists, and children of police officers who died on job. The number of recommendations is limited and sparse. Then, how did Colleague Zhu's daughter manage to get the recommendation?

Qiqi looked at Colleague Zhu in front of her, who was filled with pride. She understood what Colleague Zhu meant. Based on Colleague Zhu's values and social outlook, she would think that a university ranked 2nd in the country would be better than a university ranked 4th in the country. Colleague Zhu thought that her daughter was better than Qiqi's daughter, and she certainly deserved to be proud. Qiqi couldn't stand her arrogance and stopped asking.

Qiqi had no intention to compete with Colleague Zhu as her excellence couldn't be matched by regular people. She had a copy of the best degree from Jinghua University. Her relatives were so outstanding that her uncle had met the Vice Premier face to face. Qiqi remained silent and didn't disclose it to her colleagues. As the popular saying goes, "Kind people are deceived by others; kind horses are ridden by others." That's why Qiqi was bullied and suppressed. Qiqi knew that she had met a low-quality person. Nevertheless, it was more important to figure out how Colleague Zhu's daughter was exempted from taking the NCEE and obtained recommendation to attend university. Not only did it involve Qiqi's family, but it also involved the students that were taking the NCEE and the fairness of education. What is more, it involved the students who had been studying day and night for the examination and the students that were ruthlessly eliminated from the fierce competition in the NCEE. Qiqi had to find out what happened behind the scenes for justice!

Qiqi was calm and quiet with no words when she met Colleague Zhu again. Colleague Zhu also felt awkward ambience, she looked at Qiqi and turned frightened.

Qiqi decided to ask her colleague first. Her colleague told Qiqi that the only information she heard from Colleague Zhu herself was that her daughter was admitted to university through recommendation from a foreign language school and tested by separate examination held in the university. Her daughter didn't take the hard NCEE. Qiqi's colleague also found it strange because they had never heard of this admission way. Most people took the NCEE and passed the examination to gain admissions into university. They wondered how Colleague Zhu knew a such admission method and even got it in one hit!

Yanjing University is ranked the 2nd in the country. It is on par with the best university in the country – Jinghua University. Qiqi wondered why such an admission way existed in education System. The admission method is easy as students only need to be tested in separate examination by university for a few subjects without intense competing as in the national unified examination. Qiqi expounded the strange case to Clear and asked her to recall if she had ever heard of this admission way through foreign language school recommendation. Clear affirmed that she had never heard of it. Her school and teachers had only talked about three types of recommendations: winners of the Olympiad, sports medalists, and children of the police officers who died on job. She had never heard of other type of recommendation. Qiqi found it strange that no one had heard about it, yet there was a real-life example case. Plus, it was declared out by Colleague Zhu herself. Maybe no one would know about it if Colleague Zhu had never revealed it.

Qiqi constantly searched for the word "foreign language school" in her mind. Qiqi wasn't a local in this metropolitan city. She had never seen a foreign language school in this city and didn't know where it was. Qiqi recalled that she had seen a foreign language school in her hometown, "Yes, it exists." Qiqi tried to recall the scene from twenty years ago, and she hadn't forgotten about it. She even asked her parents about it, and both her parents told her that they didn't know about the existence of foreign language school. During university, Qiqi's father was a class monitor and had classmates coming from all over the country. Even so, her dad didn't know about the existence of the foreign language school.

The more Qiqi thought about it, the more unbelievable it became that her elders, contemporaries, her daughter etc., they didn't know about foreign language school. How did Colleague Zhu know about it? Qiqi pondered and recalled the embarrassing scene when she asked about Colleague Zhu's degree. At that time, Colleague Zhu was very reluctant to answer. Qiqi knew that if she were to ask Colleague Zhu about her daughter's recommended admission to university, she would refuse to answer. The Times had entered 21st century and it was the age of science and technology where the Internet was available, Qiqi would be able to find clues as there was a lot of information on the Internet.

Qiqi went online and used a certain application to search for "foreign language school recommendations." The results were out! Qiqi clapped her hands and wanted to scold herself for being simple-minded. Although the information on the Internet was scattered, Qiqi understood what happened after browsing the Internet. The truth! The truth could be found on the Internet! Qiqi was thankful that people wouldn't be beclouded anymore in the age of science and technology. She cheered in her heart!

CHAPTER ELEVEN

The Education Department

Qiqi spent more than ten days scouring the Internet repeatedly, checking through various resources and comments. Finally, the truth was slowly revealed.

It turned out to be a special operation by the education department in order to cater to the upper class. This arrangement undermines the fair competition widely promoted by the education department as it bypasses the competition through the NCEE and may cause public anger among students and parents of regular schools. Hence, it has always been operating separately with secrecy, and such benefit is only conferred to foreign language school students and not to the public. This results in the lack of awareness among the public that there is such a way to gain admission to university.

Foreign language schools were established in the 1950s and 1960s and have been in existence for nearly 70 years. There are 16 foreign language schools in large cities, with only 1 or 2 such schools in each city.

The type of education taught in foreign language schools is middle school education. It mainly accepts students from junior middle school level. Affiliated elementary schools were also established as well. On the surface, foreign language schools accept students from all over the city. But since there are affiliated elementary schools, foreign language schools do not need to worry about not having enough students, let alone to publicize admissions widely.

Oh yes! When Qiqi saw the information on the Internet, suddenly she recalled the scene where she discovered the existence of a foreign language school in a secluded area when she was going to the bookstore. At that time, she even wondered, "What's the purpose of foreign language school?" Piecing all the information together, Qiqi realized why the school was built in a secluded area, where it was half-hidden by the tall sycamore trees. It was also their special meaning: Don't want to be known by too many people.

Qiqi wanted to know why the education department established foreign language schools and what students' study in those schools. What is the difference between the students in foreign language schools and students in regular schools?

In addition to the main foreign languages such as English and Russian, foreign language schools also offer a wide range of language courses in minor foreign languages such as Japanese, Korean, Arabic, Hebrew, German, French, etc. The school focuses on training the ability of students to communicate in a foreign language, i.e., to be able to speak fluently in daily expression and communicate with foreigners.

Qiqi understood. Foreign language schools are set up to communicate with foreigners. Qiqi stopped and recalled the memories she had about regular high schools that most people had attended. Regular high schools would teach foreign languages too, it is English. English is recognized as a universal language and is widely used worldwide. It is also a very important subject in middle school and one of the compulsory subjects in the NCEE. Both the school and students attached great importance to studying English. The best proof was seen during Clear's high school years, where the English teacher once instructed all the students to read the English texts up to fifteen times.

It is a clear violation of social fairness as regular students who learned English had to compete fiercely in the NCEE for a chance to go to university, while foreign language school students who studied minor foreign languages could easily go to university without taking unified examination. Students in normal middle schools may not be able to enter university even after studying hard for more than ten years. But the education department uses its authority and power, grants numerous recommendations to attend universities to foreign language school students generously as if the recommendation were an ordinary item. Such different treatment would cause public anger among students and families in regular middle schools.

No wonder Qiqi's daughter did not receive relevant paper notice from the local educational organizations before going to junior middle school. It turned out that students did not have to attend junior middle school in nearby designated public schools.

Comments on the Internet talked about it, foreign language schools are also public middle schools, they mainly started to recruit students at the junior middle school level. The foreign language schools received students citywide, it meant that when entering junior middle school, the city students could also choose to attend a foreign language school. But in fact, the foreign language schools often quietly displayed their admissions information on their school web pages. Many students and families didn't receive verbal notice or paper notice, they were less aware of the existence of that school, let alone the favorable treatment for attending university one would receive in the future.

Yes, the information on the Internet was right! Qiqi remembered. The general public, who was honest and unsuspecting, believed in the government, what they received were merely verbal message.

"Students would be assigned to the nearby public middle school by sortition." Such an arrangement was equivalent to assigning school!

The information on the Internet also showed that foreign language schools were established in the 1950s and 1960s. At that time, the country needed to carry out external communication and elevate its international standing to obtain international support. Hence, the propaganda department of the country hoped that the education department would train foreign language personnel for foreign relations.

In order to cater to the upper class, The education department established foreign language schools separately in addition to regular high schools and operated alone so regular students and parents wouldn't be aware of it clearly, forming an information barrier. Moreover, the education department issued many recommendations to attend university to the 16 foreign language schools six months in advance of the NCEE. There are more than 1,600 foreign language school students who have obtained the recommendations to attend university every year. They account for many of all types of recommendations.

Qiqi thought, the education department is acting against the spirit of indenture. For a long time, the education department has been widely promoting the way to qualify for university through the NCEE. Almost every family and student regarded it as a government rule. However, the education department is operating behind the public, sacrificing the numerous fair opportunities for education belonging to the people. This duplicity has existed for decades! It was pathetic that the students in regular high schools had to devote their time to the Olympiad competition. They are constantly thinking about problems even when they are walking. But in return, only a small number of recommendations are given to the Olympiad students. Which is more important? Which students are better? The education department is so biased towards foreign language school students that they disregard justice and fairness.

The information on the Internet also showed the number of college admissions is limited, and it is impossible for universities to admit students without a limit. **The foreign language school**

students receive their university admissions half a year in advance. More than 1,000 university admissions reserved for NCEE students will be reduced. In other words, more than 1,000 innocent students will be sacrificed every year!

Qiqi realized that the consequences of such action by the education department had deeply harmed social justice. As the economy and technology are developing, the job market in this country values higher education very much, especially degree holders. Having a degree equates to having a ticket to a job and a stable income. Without a degree, there are no good job opportunities as one cannot earn enough to survive and will suffer in poverty and lowliness. This is a cruel fact that everyone is aware of in real life. To guarantee people's basic right to survive, having a degree is everyone's real right to survive. Such a ruthless operation by the education department will make people lose trust in them as Qiqi no longer trust the education department anymore.

In retrospect, how did Colleague Zhu know that there is such a way to gain admission to university? Not only did she know about it, but she also managed to help her daughter achieve success?

Qiqi recalled all the clues and traces of Colleague Zhu's behavior ever since she met her, filtering through every detail. Suddenly, she remembered the case when she and her colleague asked Colleague Zhu about her major. Qiqi could vividly recall the strange look on Colleague Zhu's face as she was reticent and was reluctant to reveal anything about her major. At that time, Qiqi was puzzled as having a degree from a formal university is a kind of achievement. Why did Colleague Zhu seem reluctant to talk about it? Colleague Zhu took foreign language as her major. The information on the internet showed that those students who are recommended by foreign language schools would usually take a foreign language as their major, and that is the unique feature for them. Suddenly, Qiqi made bold conjecture: Did Colleague Zhu obtain her foreign language degree through the NCEE? Or did she obtain her degree without competing in the NCEE?

Motivated by the idea, Qiqi jumped up excitedly. She couldn't help but praise herself for being smart. The only answer to all the strange events was that Colleague Zhu herself was a student at a foreign language school and was admitted to university with recommendation. She didn't take the NCEE just like her daughter! In other words, her family members must have relied on this way to get their degrees!

This explains why Colleague Zhu's daughter was able to hit the bull's eye and enter a prestigious university because Colleague Zhu had personally experienced it. She must have been aware of the tips and tricks and given her daughter a lot of guidance in advance. As the saying goes, "awkward on the first try, but skillful later on the second try." That is the main reason why her daughter was able to enter the 2nd excellent university in the country. Qiqi nodded in admiration: Colleague Zhu's daughter took the examination with the wisdom of two heads.

Exam, exam? Qiqi wondered. Based on the arrangement of the education department, the foreign language school students would have obtained recommendations to attend university. Why did Colleague Zhu's daughter take an examination before entering university? Didn't she get the recommendation to attend university? Qiqi was confused and could only continue to search for clues online.

She sighed when she saw the search results popping up as she scoured the Internet. She was grateful that she was able to find out the truth through the Internet with the advent of science and technology. Where else could she discover the truth if not for the Internet?

The education department is the governing agency for all the universities across the country. All the universities could only obey the education department's orders. The foreign language school students were not good at all subjects, as they were not examined by the rigorous NCEE. On the Internet, some insiders even revealed the actual situation in foreign language schools: Many students are relaxed during the 1st and 2nd years of high school. They only took things seriously and practiced their oral language in their senior year when they were due for graduation test. For them, anyway, it is easy to go to university with recommendation.

The foreign language school students are often lackadaisical in university. The situation became more and more serious over time and eventually affected the reputation of the university, many universities were reluctant to accept the recommended foreign language school students. So, the education department agreed to allow universities to test with a few subjects for foreign language students who had already obtained recommendations. The examination is not unified examination, it is separate examination organized by each university. The foreign language school students only need to take a few subjects in the separate examination. Moreover, the number of students taking the separate examination is limited to foreign language students **only** as other students are not allowed to participate.

Qiqi had to praise the education department's painstaking efforts to come up with such a well-crafted arrangement: For universities to accept the recommended students, the students are given a few subjects during separate examination, so they won't be rejected by universities. On paper, the operation seems fair. Also, if the special operation causes public outcry, the education department can suppress it by saying that the students are tested.

It was an artifice to change the quality and substance of examination, the education department replaced unified examination with separate examination to feign as excellence.

Qiqi was very resentful: The assessment from unified written test cannot be replaced casually, the substitution is not exact.

Qiqi's Battle

Qiqi was so depressed that she wasn't herself for many days. She became sluggish and lifeless. The education department's actions had made Qiqi doubt the administration departments: Do they really care about the public? Or do they put their interests on top of the public? Growing up, the country had always encouraged the public to be patriotic by educating their people. But what about the administration departments? Do they really love the people? It seems to be uncertain.

Qiqi was a careful person. She thought that she needed to verify her speculations on Colleague Zhu's degree. What other ways could Qiqi verify the truth since Colleague Zhu was reluctant to talk about her degree? She couldn't ask her colleagues either because they might not know about it. Plus, it involved Colleague Zhu's personal privacy, and she wouldn't disclose it easily. Qiqi recalled that Colleague Zhu had a good relationship with the department head. Colleague Zhu might conceal the source of her degree to other colleagues, but she wouldn't conceal it in front of the upper superior.

Qiqi saw the document issued by the education department online, the department document clearly pointed out work arrangement after college graduation for those students who received recommended university admissions by foreign language schools. The department document required "Related-work should be arranged to according to their college major as much as possible."

Qiqi knew, Colleague Zhu majored in a foreign language, but her current job was commodity management role and did not require oral communication in foreign language. At most, her job just needed reading some literal foreign language on a few documents.

Qiqi decided to submit a proposal to the upper management to suggest that jobs should be arranged according to their college majors. For instance, Colleague Zhu should be working on jobs related to her major, and adjustments should be made.

Qiqi worked in a department responsible for reviewing the commodity information submitted by the companies, and the department head was a lady. Qiqi once heard the superior lady complained about her trouble in financial situation. She had a home mortgage and a car loan. Her financial situation was difficult.

Qiqi guessed that Colleague Zhu must have had a good relationship with the lady superior. Because her work role was very important in the department. Based on the submission procedure, Qiqi's proposal would be rejected if she were to submit her proposal to this lady superior. Qiqi pondered and decided to praise the lady superior in the final part of the proposal. She added a few sentences to praise the lady superior for being fair.

After that, Qiqi prepared herself sensibly and went to the superior's office on a weekday morning. She submitted the proposal to the lady superior formally and waited at the next table. Qiqi's proposal had about 2,000 words and was almost five-page long. It would take a while for the superior to read.

The lady superior was Geng by surname. She sat in office seat and started reading Qiqi's proposal. Just a little while, she panicked and wanted to question Qiqi. But Qiqi suggested: "Continue reading; you can ask me questions after you finish. I'll wait."

Superior Geng started to flip through the proposal and read the contents quickly. She was in a state of obvious panic, and her body was shaking abnormally because of the nervous emotion. Qiqi looked at her reaction, surprised to see her acting like that and wondered: "Why she was so nervous?" Once Superior Geng finished reading, she quickly threw the proposal aside and ran fast to Qiqi anxiously. While running, she blurted out in panic, "What do you want?"

Qiqi was very surprised as she didn't expect such a strange response from Superior Geng. The response seems to be done in exchange, it's like doing transaction.

A strange feeling came out from Qiqi's heart: This is the Commodity Management Bureau, and it is a clean government agency. The unit had always promoted incorruptibility among the staff. How could there be such philistine answer? It seemed that there was something wrong with Superior Geng.

After sorting out her thoughts, Qiqi explained concisely. She felt that assigning jobs based on university majors could make the best use of the staff 's talents. This arrangement was more reasonable and was better for the unit. Superior Geng waved her hand decisively arrogantly and said that it was not up to Qiqi to decide. She paused for a while as she realized that what she said had crossed the line. Then, she spoke in a softer tone and started to persuade Qiqi not to be involved in Colleague Zhu's matters. Qiqi was unmoved and insisted on submitting the proposal. After that, Superior Geng tried to persuade her for a long time. Qiqi understood her intention to shield Colleague Zhu, Qiqi answered firmly, "I can send the proposal to the unit chat group." Superior Geng stopped persuading, and her face was glum. During the conversation, Qiqi realized the truth of the matter, Colleague Zhu was admitted to university without taking the NCEE, OK! Qiqi left with the gained message.

Qiqi dug out the final truth! Colleague Zhu obtained her degree without taking the NCEE. She was admitted to university through recommendation by foreign language school. Her daughter followed her footsteps and used the same way to gain the benefit of entering a top university. Obviously, it is opportunistic, both avoided the mainstream way to attend university (the NCEE), they got recommendations to attend university by same special path; they profited family members with prophetic information; just like in stock trading, one could have insider news and prepared in advance to gain huge profits and benefits. For generations, it was evident that the family members of Colleague Zhu obtained degrees through the special way to avoid national unified examination.

Now, Qiqi understood why Colleague Zhu was reluctant to talk about her degree back then. It was because the NCEE is difficult, and the admission quota to university is limited. Not many people would be able to pass the NCEE and gain admissions to excellent university. Those who are admitted are praised as "Heaven's Favor" and valued by society. In addition to good job opportunities and benefits, they would also be assigned to important roles and prioritized for promotions and salary increments in later stages. All these are the value of the NCEE. Society places importance on the prestige of the NCEE and degrees obtained through the examination. This is widely recognized by the whole society. Of course, Colleague Zhu knew very well that the reality of society values degrees obtained through the NCEE. Her degree was acquired through special means. In other words, her grades in high school weren't good at many subjects, and she didn't pass through the unified examination (the NCEE). In strict terms, she didn't gain a real admission to attend university; she was "sent" to the university by the education department through special arrangements. Hence, she was reluctant to talk about her degree, her degree was discounted in value. She kept silence because she wanted to pretend that she obtained her degree by taking the NCEE. She wanted to take advantage of other's ignorance to continue to gain relevant benefits.

Qiqi thought: Colleague Zhu is neither smart nor has a high IQ and EQ. After her daughter used the same way to enter university and achieved great success, Colleague Zhu was overwhelmed with joy and victory. She was carried away and felt that she could win and oppress Qiqi as her daughter got the 2nd excellent university, much better than Qiqi's daughter, who only got 4th excellent university in the country. Colleague Zhu considered herself that she was the biggest winner with her daughter!

Qiqi couldn't help but laugh when she thought of people like Colleague Zhu, those who thought themselves clever and wanted to pretend to be good. Perhaps, no one around them had ever been admitted to a prestigious university?

Qiqi recalled the best degree from Jinghua University that she had stored alongside her all these years. The degree belonged to Qiqi's classmate, who studied hard for many years. It was Qiqi's own excellence that this best degree accompanied her.

Qiqi contemplated whether she should reveal the best degree to everyone or continue to keep it hidden and bury its precious brilliance.

With Qiqi's elite upbringing, she didn't want to reveal it as it would be seen as showing off and may cause a strong blow to others because no one's degree would be better than that degree, and everyone would be ashamed. Feeling embarrassed, Qiqi couldn't think of any other way and decided to put the matter aside.

For the next few days, Qiqi couldn't help but recall the strange reaction and discouragement from Superior Geng when she submitted the work proposal to her that day. Looking back, Qiqi finally understood that all these were only the tip of the iceberg.

Superior Geng valued power and authority at work. Modifying information on documents is a task with a lot of flexibility given to the ratifier. This work had been previously approved by the deputy superior of the department, but it was often approved by Superior Geng. She had the power on modification of information on documents. The data information could be modified with her signature and consent. Hence, the business companies would apply her for permission if they wanted to modify the commodity information. Superior Geng tried her best to protect Colleague Zhu because the work process required two person's signatures at least, and Colleague Zhu was a coagent. Colleague Zhu should know something about Superior Geng in revising the document information, Colleague Zhu was an insider. Qiqi realized that her work proposal must have been written in vain! Even if Superior Geng submitted the work proposal based on the procedure, it wouldn't be accepted! That was because Qiqi heard that Superior Geng had someone backing her in the upper management as well, and it was a male director named Pan. He had a close relationship with Superior Geng and often stood on her side. That was one reason why Superior Geng was the head of the department for a long time.

Finally, Qiqi figured it out. No wonder Colleague Zhu was so wild and behaved so arrogantly. It turned out that she had several people from the upper management behind her. To them, Qiqi was just an ordinary colleague with no status and power. That was why they didn't take her seriously!

Feeling depressed, Qiqi paced back and forth, but she couldn't think of another way. She could only console herself. The education department could make special arrangements and sacrifice more than 1,000 NCEE students' futures. Superior Geng shielding her coagent was nothing compared to that.

The feeling of depression enveloped Qiqi. She felt oppressed. Moments later, a sense of justice emanated from heart, and she decided to do her bit to uphold fairness and justice in society.

Qiqi took a picture of the copy of the degree from Jinghua University that she had stored for all these years. Then she sent it to the unit chat group and showed it to everyone, explaining that it was a degree from the best university, and it was obtained through the NCEE with excellent grades, not through special means.

At the same time, the news was out in the unit that Qiqi had submitted a work proposal to the upper management. When Qiqi met Colleague Zhu again, Colleague Zhu lowered her head with obvious shame.

In the evening, Qiqi was watching TV at home and saw some news reports related to her hometown. She sighed and recalled that she hadn't returned to her hometown for a long time. She recalled the memories of her hometown and her ex-colleagues. Looking back, she suddenly remembered the hula hoop contestant who studied in an excellent university, majoring in a foreign language. Everything was clear now, and Qiqi figured out the strange things that she had never understood before: The hula hoop contestant must have entered university through recommendation by foreign language school. She must have obtained her degree without taking the NCEE.

There must be some reasons why she didn't want to have children. In addition to superficial reasons such as time and energy spent during childbirth and difficulty in raising children, there was a hidden reason: Once she has children, her children will have to face the giant hurdle that is the NCEE in the future. It would be difficult for her children to enter excellent universities if they were to take the NCEE. If they decided to avoid the NCEE, then the only solution was to enter foreign language school, that would expose the origin of her degree! For instance, Colleague Zhu's origin of degree was exposed because her daughter took after her and attended a top university without the written test of unified examination.

Ah, Qiqi sighed. What a cunning degree!

– COMPLETE –

Clear and Mum

Acknowledgment

I wish to convey my sincere thanks to every righteous reader and my supporters. The creation of this book came largely from immense dedication and perseverance. Many thanks to my daughter, Clear Chen, and the information provided by the Internet which is a great help to gather info for this book. Final thanks to the support and assistance provided by Asian Culture Press for publishing and distributing this book.

Because I have lived in a country where the official language is not English for a long time, the use of English is relatively unfamiliar, there may be inaccurate words, I hope the readers understand, thank you!

Pretty Qi

www.ingramcontent.com/pod-product-compliance
Lightning Source LLC
Chambersburg PA
CBHW030645190726
48286CB00008B/2666